I0712743

Just One Family

The Billionaire Barons of Texas ∾ Book Nine

CHRIS KENISTON

Indie House Publishing

This book is a work of fiction. Names, characters, places and incidents are the product of the author's imagination or are used fictionally. Any resemblance to actual events, locales, or persons, living or dead, is coincidental.

Copyright 2024 Christine Baena
Print Edition

Indie House Publishing

MORE BOOKS
By Chris Keniston

The Billionaire Barons of Texas
Just One Date
Just One Spark
Just One Dance
Just One Take
Just One Taste
Just One Shot
Just One Chance
Just One Mistake
Just One Family
Just One Rodeo
Just One Surprise
Just One Look

Hart Land
Heather
Lily
Violet
Iris
Hyacinth
Rose
Calytrix
Zinnia
Poppy
Picture Perfect

Farraday Country
Adam
Brooks
Connor
Declan
Ethan

Finn
Grace
Hannah
Ian
Jamison
Keeping Eileen
Loving Chloe
Morgan
Neil
Owen
Paxton

Honeymoon Series
Honeymoon for One
Honeymoon for Three
Honeymoon for Four
Honeymoon for Five
Honeymoon for Six
Honeymoon for Seven

Aloha Romance Series:
Aloha Texas
Almost Paradise
Mai Tai Marriage
Dive Into You
Look of Love
Love by Design
Love Walks In
Shell Game
Flirting with Paradise

Surf's Up Flirts:
(Aloha Series Companions)
Shall We Dance
Love on Tap
Head Over Heels
Perfect Match
Just One Kiss
It Had to Be You
Cat's Meow

CHAPTER ONE

The breathtaking views of Houston's skyline were the only thing helping Leah Baron keep her sanity this afternoon. That, and the prospect of spending the weekend at the family ranch.

Her fingers rapidly tapped at the keys of her laptop, her gaze shifted from one screen to another. She'd spent a small fortune on the ergonomic leather chair specifically for days like today that didn't want to come to an end. Thank heaven she stood her ground and insisted on taking advanced typing instead of chemistry back in high school or she'd be hunting and pecking at the keys till sunrise tomorrow in an effort to finish this blasted brief.

As much as she needed to get through this before moving on to the remaining paperwork sprawled across her desk, her phone buzzing was a welcome interruption. Maybe. Glancing at the screen, she saw a familiar contact— her baby sister, Rachel. Leah swiped to answer, multitasking effortlessly.

"You are missing all the fun!" Excitement frosted every word out of Rachel's mouth.

Leah sighed. Fun was a way of life at Paradise Ridge. Any day of the week she'd rather be there than sitting behind a massive mahogany desk that the partners insisted on when they assigned her the corner office. Then again, she did love the law, just not the paperwork that came with it. "What's going on?"

"Mitch's latest equine acquisition, his prize stud, escaped the stables. Claire told him that the family needed to have better stalls for a stallion of that stamina but it looks like everyone is going to learn their lesson the hard way.

Mack is out running an errand and it only took Craig, Devlin, and Porter two hours to catch the guy. I won't tell you how long it took to get him back into the stall."

Holding back her mirth, Leah shook her head. "I assume no one was injured in this little escapade?"

"Only their egos."

The Barons were known for many things, being stubborn was on the top of the list. Of course, that was just one of the attributes that boosted success for every generation no matter their career choice. Though, honestly, she thought Mitch was the most reasonable of all her siblings and cousins so the fact that he didn't listen to her veterinarian sister Claire was a surprise. "Anything else?"

"Actually, yes. Mom is looking for a headcount on who is going to attend tomorrow night's opening of the new exhibit for the Art Museum sponsored by the Baron Foundation. Apparently, there's a seating issue and Grams wants to make sure that the top donors get stellar status."

"So, does that mean she does or doesn't want as many Barons as possible to schmooze donors out of their money?"

"Your guess is as good as mine. But there's something else."

The conspiratorial whisper in her sister's voice made Leah wish she was in the same room with Rachel, not on the phone. "Is this going to make my day or have me tossing my laptop across the room?"

"If I'm right, it might make your year."

That build-up had her pulling her hands away from the keyboard and sitting back in the mostly comfortable chair, listening intently to what her sister had to say next. "I'm listening."

"You know how Gwyneth has been a little under the weather the last few weeks?"

Leah nodded before it struck her that her sister couldn't see her. "Yes. But she tested negative for Covid, and even if I didn't already know she wasn't positive, that wouldn't be good news. To make my year you'd have to tell me something way more interesting like she's...oh my lord."

The dots quickly connected in her mind. Besides not feeling up to snuff, Gwyneth was drinking ginger ale all the time. Leah had assumed it was because she'd been fighting a bug but now… "She's pregnant!" It wasn't really a question.

"Shh. Someone might hear you."

Leah actually looked around to see who might hear, even though she knew darn well she was the only person in her office and those walls were soundproof enough to have a hard rock band practice without disturbing the other offices. Even so, Leah whispered, "I'm right, aren't I?"

Since it took a few moments for Rachel to respond, Leah knew, just like she'd done a moment ago, her kid sister was either nodding or shaking her head. "Sorry. Yes. But I wasn't supposed to overhear her telling Grams and the Governor. She and Mitch want to make the announcement this weekend at supper."

"Oh, how exciting for Mitch! It doesn't surprise me at all that they would want to start a family right away. This is so cool." Leah could hardly contain her joy for her cousin. The man had been so devastated when he lost his first wife and had mentioned more than once how he regretted that they had put off having children until his career didn't take him away from home so often. Staring at the words on her computer, she wanted to chuck the dumb thing and grab all her siblings and cousins and celebrate the good news. "The Governor must be thrilled to finally get a new generation of Barons on the way."

"Too thrilled. He's already barked at Chase and Kyle for lagging behind."

Smiling, Leah shook her head. So like her grandfather to go into Marine mode. "The man does understand that having a family isn't quite the same as ordering a pizza?"

"Actually, Kyle said something very similar." Rachel laughed. "I think rather than take the heat off of the rest of us, this is only going to fan the flames."

"Great." Sarcasm rolled off her tongue. "Guess I'll have to move having a family up a few rows on my bucket list."

Rachel barked out a laugh. "You do that. And most definitely do not miss dinner on Sunday. It's going to be a blast."

"Got it." She disconnected the call with her sister and stared at the screen. She was smiling so hard her face started to hurt. Rachel was absolutely right, this was the best news she'd had all year. Blowing out a sigh, she looked at a notepad on her desk. Maybe putting having a family of her own on her to-do list wasn't such a bad idea at all?

Logan Miller looked down at his watch. This day was going from long to longer, and he feared he was never going to get out of here. The low hum of the office air conditioning provided little comfort as the muted glow of his computer screen cast a tired reflection in his eyes. Even the coveted view of the San Francisco bay did nothing to improve his mood.

Deleting spam email, one after another, one subject line caught his attention: "Important Announcement Regarding Company Relocation." Logan's stomach tightened with an unsettling tincture of curiosity and dread. Clicking open the message, he read about the company's strategic decision to move its headquarters from California to Texas—*Texas*. Acid churned in his gut. The rumors of a major move out of state were coming to pass. Reading on, the memo cited financial advantages to both employer and employees as well as the more business-friendly environment the move would provide, citing improved cost of living, housing, stellar schools, and, of course, the beloved lack of state income tax. Add a song and dance routine and it would make a great commercial for relocation company.

The words blurred together as Logan absorbed the implications. A move to halfway across the country. His life was in California. He'd been born and bred in the bay area. All his friends, and what little family he had left, all lived somewhere in Northern California. Not that he had a whole lot of time to see any of them, but knowing he had a support system if he needed them, or if they needed him, gave him some semblance of comfort. The idea of uprooting everything felt daunting.

His gaze drifted to a photo on his desk. A small hammer inside his skull began to bang out the beginnings of a nasty headache. Somehow he'd have to explain this career move to a lot of unhappy people.

Just as Logan tried to wrap his head around the life-altering news and the collateral damage, his boss, Mr. Reynolds, appeared at his office doorway. The older man wore a forced smile that failed to reach his eyes.

"Logan, I need you in the conference room," Mr. Reynolds's tone held a mix of formality and reluctance.

Entering the conference room, Logan found himself surrounded by tense faces. The air felt heavy with anticipation as Mr. Reynolds began the presentation, emphasizing the positive aspects of the relocation—lower taxes, reduced cost of living, and improved overall profitability. Logan tried to focus on the charts and graphs, but his mind drifted back and forth to glimpses of the world he'd be leaving behind.

"Logan, you'll be part of the first wave heading to Houston," Mr. Reynolds's announcement snapped him back to the present. "Your flight leaves Monday morning. We need you to oversee the initial transition."

Nodding, he did his best to conceal the whirlwind of emotions beneath a stoic exterior. As the meeting continued, he couldn't shake the sense of displacement that settled over him. As his boss continued to speak, shock and dread slid aside as reality and panic settled in. Monday was only five days away. Who packed up an entire life in only five days?

"Of course," Mr. Reynolds continued, "the company will cover all relocation costs, and a hefty bonus will be included with your relocation package."

While the idea of a bonus sounded like a good thing, he wasn't sure it was good enough to justify uprooting his whole world.

"We've booked moving companies to pack everyone up, and transport your belongings to Houston. We've also assigned a relocation realtor to help find housing. Any questions?"

Only a million, but none of which would be appropriate in this setting. Instead, he shook his head.

"Well, if you need any more information, you know where to find me."

Again, Logan nodded. None of this seemed real. He had enough trouble finding matching socks in the morning, how was he going to manage a change like this, moving company or not, packing a lifetime was only the tip of the iceberg when it came to upending his world. But like it or not, he had a good job with an even better future. He simply couldn't afford to say no and find himself looking for a new job.

No, he was going to have to suck it up and make the best of it. After all, maybe Texas wouldn't be a bad place. Maybe?

CHAPTER TWO

Since nobody in the family was supposed to know about Mitch and Gwyneth's news, Leah had to refrain from buying out the toy store before Sunday dinner. Now that everybody knew, there was no reason she couldn't begin indulging her new niece or nephew ahead of the rest of the family. On her to do list for the day, somewhere between picking up her dry-cleaning and having her car washed, she now added a trip to the mall.

Eager to peruse the specialty toy store, Leah managed to pick up her dry-cleaning in record time, returned to her house and hung the clean clothes in her closet so her linen skirts wouldn't wrinkle. That done, she darted back out to the mall. A message from her boss on a recent case meant she'd have to skip the car wash and head back to the office, but nothing was getting in the way of shopping for the newest member of the family.

Not bothering with the madhouse referred to as a parking lot, she pulled up to the valet and made her way inside. It had been ages since she had time to visit the mall. She really did need to find a bit more balance in her life. A strong work ethic was genetically tattooed in the Baron DNA, but for the first time in a long time, Sunday supper with all the family celebrating Mitch and Gwyneth had Leah beginning to think that maybe she was just missing out on a little bit more of life than she really should. After all, she didn't have to be a race car driver like her cousin Kyle or a movie producer rubbing elbows with A-list stars of Hollywood like Craig, but working eighty to a hundred and twenty hours a week might be a bit much. Today's message was an excellent case in point. Maybe if her partners were used to her taking time off for an island vacation or shopping in Paris, her phone wouldn't buzz at all hours of the day or night.

Ever since meeting her sister Rachel's husband—well, he wasn't her husband when Leah met him—but ever since getting to know Dylan, bit by bit, the idea that life wasn't all about work had started to take root. Preparing for a new niece or nephew was just the sort of distraction she needed to start helping her work towards finding more balance. And a late morning lost in the toy store was the perfect start to her new endeavor to be the best aunt any kid ever had. Maybe she should just text back that she'd get to it on Monday.

As for the idea of best aunt award, the challenge was where to begin. She really didn't have a clue about shopping for babies. She'd never babysat as a teen, and worked too much to keep up with her friends who were raising kids. Where so many of her friends dreamed of marrying and having children, Leah dreamed of arguing a case in front of the Supreme Court, not in front of a wayward teen and their school principal.

Not that she expected Mitch and Gwyneth's offspring to become a problem child, but for now, she needed to quit ruminating on life choices and focus on a gift for the little one. The stuffed animals were precious, but didn't those cause allergies or something like that? Dolls had come a long way since she was a kid. A couple of times she had to do a double take, they looked so realistic, but of course that was impractical for an infant and even more so if her niece turned out to be a nephew. This little shopping adventure was much more challenging than she'd anticipated. One thing was for sure, she was sorely out of touch with the world of babies. Maybe she would need to do more research. That was it. If research worked in the legal world, it certainly made sense it would work in the world of babies and children.

Standing in the aisle with a plethora of children's books, she spotted a section on baby books. The kind for tracking firsts. Some were more complex than others, some were more frilly, but one in particular caught her eye. It wasn't over the top fancy, but it wasn't austere either. There were places to write down trivial things and important things. At least she assumed how much babies ate and slept was important. As someone who worked with files all day, she got a kick out of the pockets for papers and other items deemed worthy of saving. Definitely a keeper, she pulled the boxed book off the shelf and continued perusing the store, aisle by aisle.

Clutching the book to her chest, she went into overload mode going through the car seat and stroller section. Good grief, buying a new car was easier than picking out a car seat. Suddenly, a law career seemed so much easier than parenthood. Moving on, she wandered by the bassinets and sleepwear. Heavens, were these little pajamas and sleepers absolutely adorable. Unable to resist, she picked up two of her favorites in yellows and pastel greens. Nice, neutral colors. She sure hoped Mitch and Gwyneth weren't going to be the kind of parents who wanted to wait until the birth to find out the baby's gender. Leah wanted to know if she was going to be buying cute clothes with ribbons and lace in pink or baseball caps and jeans in shades of blue.

Reaching the end of the aisle, holding her book and two pajamas, she noticed a cute little girl walking past her. Leah wasn't a great judge of children's ages, but she thought the girl was too young to be shopping on her own. This sort of thing happened all the time in the grocery store. Some parent would leave their kids playing in the toy or candy aisle or worse, let them run all over the store while mom or dad shopped. Leah supposed a toy store was heaven for little kids, but she really wished these parents paid more attention.

Back at the stuffed animal section where she started, Leah decided to hell with allergies. The cutest little gray kitty caught her eye. Not boy or girl, not too big to smother, and most likely just the right size for a growing infant to hug. Yep, her first gifts would be practical and cute. Content with her purchases, she went straight to the cashier and caught sight of that same little girl hovering just outside the front door of the store. Where was her mother or father? Glancing left then right, she didn't see anyone even remotely nearby who looked to be a parent. Turning, she looked inside the store. Again, no one seemed to be looking for a child. What was the matter with people nowadays?

She may not be in a hurry to have kids of her own, or know a whole lot about raising kids, but any idiot should know better than to leave a cute little girl wandering around a mall on her own. Already on her way to where the little girl stood, determined to find the careless parent, she was taken by surprise when the girl met her halfway and looked up at her.

"Do you like little girls?"

Smiling at the sweetness, Leah crouched down to the child's eye level. "Why, as a matter of fact, I do."

The little girl nodded. "I saw you buying presents."

"Yes. My cousin is having a baby."

"I like stuffed animals." The girl smiled up at her. For a second, Leah thought the child was going to ask her for a stuffed animal, but then she quickly added, "The baby will be very happy."

"I hope so." Leah smiled down at the child, casually glancing around again for a parent. Nothing.

"Would you like to be a mommy?"

That wasn't what she expected the child to say.

"Some day. Yes." Though after today's shopping experience, some day was definitely not going to be anytime soon.

"Good." The little girl rummaged in her pocket and pulling something out, opened her palm to Leah. "I have five dollars. Would you be my mommy?"

Not sure what to say, she wondered if this was some kind of prank. She actually looked around for hidden cameras or something. Obviously, it was time to take this child to security and figure out what kind of crazy—and careless—parents she had, but in the meantime, how the heck was she supposed to explain to this sweet little girl that you don't buy a mommy?

Some days Logan really wished he could have just stayed in bed. Today was definitely one of them. Coming to the mall on a Saturday felt much like taking his life into his own hands. Mothers pushing strollers while corralling a second child and running over anyone in their path followed by a meek apology as they continue plowing through the shoppers. Teens roaming packs like wild dogs. Older shoppers moseying along as if they were channeling the little old lady from Pasadena. Stopping at the overcrowded food court wasn't any easier on an overworked and harried man.

"I'm sorry." Michelle's voice softened his heart.

Maybe he was being too hard on the poor moms, bored teens, and strolling seniors. After all, some day he'd be one of those retired elderly with nothing but time on their hands. And didn't that sound just wonderful right about now. "Accidents happen. It's okay. As soon as I finish cleaning up the spilled milkshake, we'll go looking for new shoes for Trish. Sound good?"

"Sounds good." Nodding, Michelle's face brightened and somehow the mall didn't seem so bad after all.

Once they hit the shoe store and got Trish's shoes, then he…looking up at Michelle standing in front of him all alone, panic surged. Looking left, then right, he even bent over to look under the table he'd been diligently wiping clean for the last several minutes. "Where's your sister?"

"I don't know."

A million thoughts ran through his head as he frantically searched the horizon for any signs of Trish. "Did you see which way she went?" He didn't dare ask what he was thinking—did someone take her?

Michelle's arm stuck straight out, one finger pointing down one hall toward a large department store.

"Are you sure?"

Her head bobbed, and grabbing her hand, he left the wet paper towels and lunch trash on the table, practically dragging Michelle as he hurried down the hall. Scanning left and right with every step, he searched for any signs of Trish. Why didn't he put her in brighter colored clothes? Or maybe a big red bow in her hair? Anything that would make her easy to spot in a crowd. Too many times of late he'd asked himself how had he moved so far up the career ladder and yet do such stupid things like lose one precocious little girl in less than a couple of hours.

His heart was beating so hard and fast he could hear it in his ears. Too many horrible scenarios were forcing their way into his head. He had to stay calm, find a security person. That was better than running around the mall like a mad man. The mall security could lock all the exits, get more people searching, alert the stores. Now scanning in double time for Trish and security, a tiny speck of hope pinched him. Not one, but two mall police stood about ten feet away.

Scooping Michelle into his arms, he trotted briskly across the way, closing the distance. "Excuse me, I have an emergency."

The one cop with a walkie-talkie at his ear held a finger up, the other one pulled him aside. "What's the problem, sir."

"I've lost a child. A girl. Trish." The police were going to need more information. Exactly how tall was she now? Did she have on the red shirt or the pink one? At least he knew her hair and eye color. He supposed that was something. And he did carry photos on his phone.

The other officer approached, talking into the radio. "Hang on, I may have some answers." The man turned to Logan, frowning, and stared at him like a parent who was about to ground their child for the rest of their life. "Are you looking for someone?"

"Yes," he huffed. "A girl. Seven. Blonde. She's got her hair in a ponytail. Blue eyes…"

The officer held up a hand. "Name?"

"Logan Miller."

The man actually rolled his eyes at him. "Not yours. The child's."

"Trish. Patricia."

Michelle tugged at his shirt.

"In a minute, honey."

"But …" Her arm shot straight out over his shoulder. "Look."

Coming straight toward him was Trish at the hand of a tall blonde who stared daggers at him.

"Trish!" Flooded with relief, he reached the stranger in two long strides and scooped his younger daughter into his arms. "You scared me."

Having let go of Trish's hand, with a large shopping bag dangling from her elbow, the blonde crossed her arms. "If you think *she* scared you, wait till *I'm* done with you."

CHAPTER THREE

Not one but two girls. What kind of man had two children and didn't know how to keep track of them? Leah was ready to breathe fire. "Do you have any idea how dangerous a place like this can be for a little girl?"

"Trust me, you have no idea what thoughts were running through my mind."

"Well, they should have run through your mind before you let her wander off and try to buy me. What would have happened if any of the criminal element in our society had approached her with candy, or toys, or her favorite, stuffed animals?"

He frowned at her. "How do you know her favorite toys are stuffed animals, and what do you mean, buy you?"

Before she could answer, one of the two officers crouched down in front of the little girl who'd told her that her name was Trish. "Do you know this man?"

Trish nodded.

"Who is he?"

"Daddy." The girl smiled brightly.

"And is this your mommy?" the officer asked.

At the same time that Trish proudly beamed *yes*, Leah and the man holding another child with a death grip abruptly responded *no*.

The officer pushed to his feet, and still frowning, looked from Leah to the man, but said nothing.

"I'm sorry for the confusion officer, but I am her father." The man quickly pulled his billfold out of his pocket and showed it to the officer.

Nodding, the officer sighed and pushed the wallet back.

"Okay. I believe you, but the lady is right. This is no place to let kids run loose. Next time, be more careful."

"I promise you, officer, there will not be a next time."

Satisfied, the two men turned and walked away.

The man who now had both his daughters' hands held tightly in each of his, turned to Leah. "Thank you so very much for watching out for Trish."

"You're welcome, I suppose." She looked down at the kids, wondering if she was about to let that cute little girl leave with a neglectful parent to an equally neglected and probably broken down home with dirty water, limited food and who locked the kid in closets when she misbehaved. Letting out a sigh, Leah settled on she'd been a lawyer too long and seen too much of the seedy side of life. People make mistakes, even good people. That didn't mean that they were living in an episode of a dark police procedural. "She's a sweet girl. Take care of her."

He nodded. Then frowned. "What did you mean, buy you?"

"Oh, she offered me five dollars to be her mommy. I gathered her mom probably didn't let her have a toy or limited computer time or something to make her go looking for a new one." She prayed her that the kid wasn't really being locked in a closet.

"Not exactly." He blew out a deep sigh. "Again, thank you."

"Are you coming with me to buy my new shoes?" Trish looked up at her.

"I'm sorry, Trish, but I have things to do today."

"Yes, Trish," the man, whose name she didn't even know, squatted down to talk to the child at her level. That small gesture gave Leah some comfort that maybe he really wasn't a totally incompetent father. "Sweetie. This nice lady…" he paused and looked up at her and she slowly realized he was silently asking her name.

"Leah."

"Leah has things to do, but it was very nice of her to keep an eye on you when Daddy wasn't there. Which is a discussion we will have when we get home." He pushed to his feet and looked at Leah, softly muttering, "Along with buying women."

"Please?" The little girl's lower lip quivered as she stared up pleadingly at Leah.

"I—"

"Trish, what did I just say?"

The little girl blinked at her daddy and nodded, but the sad face was firmly in place.

Oh, Leah was going to be a terribly indulgent mother. How could anyone resist that face. She sighed. "I suppose I could spare a few minutes."

Trish's face brightened, and even though she hadn't met the other child before, even that little girl's face lit up as though they'd been promised a new toy every day for the rest of the year.

"Really, you don't—"

Shaking her head, Leah cut him off. "It's okay. Really. My car doesn't need washing that badly." And for sure she was now telling her partner that Monday was good enough. Unless, of course, her conscience got the better of her and not for the first time in her career, she'd spend Sunday at work not at the ranch.

The man smiled and letting go of the older girl, extended his hand. "Logan Miller."

She accepted his proffered hand. "Leah Baron."

The guy nodded, with no reaction to the family name. That had to be a first for her.

Walking a few feet in front of them, but close enough to grab on a moment's notice, the two little girls had their heads together and were whispering and giggling.

"I hope your wife won't be too upset with you." Leah kept a close eye on the girls.

"I don't have a wife anymore."

The two girls momentarily glanced over their shoulders at the adults and Leah felt this conversation was not meant for little ears. "You're d-i-v-o-r-c-e-d?"

Also keeping his gaze on the girls, without turning to face her, he responded, "W-i-d-o-w-e-r."

Leah's heart sank to her feet. She couldn't have felt

more guilty for thinking the worst of this poor man. "I'm so sorry for your loss."

"Thank you. No matter how much time passes, every day I still keep discovering new things that Deb knew or did that I didn't have a clue about. For instance, new shoes. If Trish hadn't mentioned her feet hurt, lord knows how long I'd have let her go before realizing shoes don't magically appear in a kids' closet."

"I am sorry."

"Thank you for doing this. It's nice to see the girls smiling."

How about that, the idiot was actually a nice guy.

Trish tried to buy a mother. That thought kept running through Logan's mind. He knew he could never replace Deb. Understood that every child needs their mother. He'd even tried going out on a few dates this past year, but quickly concluded that some people were only meant to have one love in their life and he'd had his. Still, somehow he thought he'd learned to make up for being a single parent. Except, according to his daughter, he was apparently failing miserably and hadn't even realized it. Though losing his baby girl should have been a thunderbolt of understanding long before learning about her shopping efforts.

"Look, Daddy." Michelle held up a pair of patent leather shoes with a heel high enough to raise more than eyebrows.

"No. You need shoes for school."

"I know." Michelle beamed. "I think they're cute."

"No," he repeated.

Leah, on the other hand, stood nodding her head. "I think I've seen those in *Vogue* magazine."

"Really?" Michelle's eyes opened wide.

On the other hand, Trish frowned. "What's *Vogue*?"

Michelle shrugged. "I don't know, but if it's in a

magazine it has to be cool."

"Sometimes yes, but I think a lot of times magazines want to sell things that real people don't wear." Leah picked up a shoe that to Logan seemed much more child-friendly. "Now, this is a cool shoe. I wish they made something like this in my size." She squeezed the inside. "I bet they're super comfortable too."

The two kids looked at each other and then Trish touched the shoe. "Do you think they come in my size?"

"We can ask. Do you want me to ask?"

Smiling, Trish bobbed her head and Michelle spun around to her father. "Can I have a new pair too?"

For a very tiny instant, he remembered what it had been like to have a partner raising the girls and squashed the ache that followed in its heels. "I think we can arrange that."

Both girls gleefully sat down in the nearest chairs, their feet swinging to and fro. He'd buy them every shoe in the place if it made them this happy all the time.

The sales clerk came out with two pairs in different colors and sizes. Each girl chose her preferred color in her size and Leah helped fit Trish while Logan fit Michelle.

"How do they feel?" Leah asked.

The girls walked away a few feet then back. "Fine," the two voices echoed.

"Let me see." Leah leaned down and pressed a finger to the toe of each shoe and nodded her head. "Room to grow. Want to walk one more time?"

The two trotted off, giggling and whispering, much the way they did whenever they played together.

Logan shifted in his seat and tore his gaze away to face Leah. "You must have children."

She shook her head. "If you mean the toe press, I remember my mother doing that when I was little. Seemed to make sense to try it now."

He chuckled softly. "Wish I remembered more of what my mom did when I was little."

"You're a boy. Perpetual motion. You probably weren't even aware of what you were doing, never mind your mother."

"The voice of experience?"

She nodded. "Two brothers and too many male cousins to count without using both our hands and feet."

"Wow." Something in the serious set of her face told him she was neither kidding nor exaggerating. "Really?"

She chuckled. "Really. My dad is one of six siblings and my uncle James had the fewest kids at only three."

"Who had the most?"

"That would be my Uncle Bradley. He has seven but it took three wives to pull it off."

All he had was two kids and he could barely manage. He didn't even want to consider if Deb had left him with five more.

Slamming their hands on each of his knees, the two girls beamed up at him. "Can we wear these home?"

"Yes, but we have to pick out another pair. No civil human being has only one pair of shoes or sheets."

"Interesting philosophy." Leah bit back a smile.

"That much I do remember my mother telling me."

"Does your mother not live nearby?"

He sighed. "No one does. We just relocated with my job. What little family we have, live in California."

"Oh. I see." The way her head bobbed and her eyes darted to the girls and back, he got the feeling she wanted to say something more, but didn't.

The next selection of shoes complete, and the shopping bags in hand, they exited the store.

"I guess this is where we part ways." Leah hunched down to speak to the girls. "I had a lovely time picking out shoes. Thank you for letting me shop with you."

"Can you come to dinner? Daddy makes really good Spaghetti-os."

Logan shook his head and cringed from the inside out. If she thought he was a lousy dad for losing his kid, not noticing she'd outgrown her shoes, and not knowing how to coax her along, feeding them Spaghetti-os probably wasn't going to bode well for him.

"I'm sorry, but I really have things to do. But thank you again."

The girls did that little pout thing that always wore him down. Too bad it didn't have the same reaction on Leah.

Straightening to her full height, Leah reached into her bag and flicked her arm at him. "Here is my business card. If you run into any more trouble, give me a call. If I can't help, I have a million relatives who will gladly step in and offer aid."

"Thank you." He accepted the card and wished he could think of something else to say that wouldn't make him sound like an idiot. "Your help is greatly appreciated."

She nodded and took a step back. "Take care of your daddy, girls." The blonde turned on her heel and walked away. Though the sleek way she passed through the crowds didn't seem at all like walking, more like gliding, or sailing, or Moses parting the Red Sea. One thing was sure, his daughter knew how to pick a nice lady.

CHAPTER FOUR

S ooner than later, Leah was going to remember to pick up a battery backup alarm clock. What good did the darn thing do if a brown out in the middle of the night reset everything? Juggling her brief case, her jacket, and the sweater that she needed to return to her office assistant, she'd closed and locked the door when she realized, no coffee.

Hurrying out the door in a fraction of the time she normally had was totally throwing her morning off. Instead of casually indulging in her first warm cup of the day as she did innocuous things like check her emails and her social media, she showered and dressed with only time for a sip or two and poured the rest into her heavy-duty, keep coffee warm travel mug. Only the mug that cost a small fortune wasn't going to do her any good sitting on the dining table.

Dropping her things at the doorway, she hurried inside, frowning when the mug wasn't where she thought she'd left it. Where the heck did she set the dumb thing down? Retracing her steps, she finally found the mug on the sink in her bathroom. With her front door open, she could hear voices. Especially that of what sounded like small children. At first it struck her as odd, and then she remembered that the apartment manager had said that they'd leased out several apartments as corporate rentals, including the one across the hall. Though the words "corporate" and "children" rarely went hand in hand, it seemed the powers that be had designated this as her week to be tripping over children.

Maybe it was fate's way of telling her it was time to slow down and perhaps even settle down. Aware now that there was more than one child in the hall after one screeched at the other over what was either a doll or a dog—Leah wasn't sure—she quickly decided no matter what fate thought, she was definitely not ready for hearth and home nor the patter of little feet. Well, maybe hearth and home wasn't so bad, but the children under foot part was another thing.

Her arms once again full, and her back to the neighbor's, she pulled her door closed and turned the lock, quickly shoving the keys in her pocket before she did something stupid like hurry away and leave them dangling from the lock.

"Hi!" an excited voice called out.

Like it or not, time to meet the neighbors. Turning slowly to not lose anything, she plastered on that polite smile all Barons had learned from an early age when forced to deal with people they really didn't want to, except instead of a strange bratty child, she was looking down at the pretty face and sweet smile of Trish from the other day.

At first she was actually pleased to see the kid, and then panic rushed through her. For the love of all that was holy, please don't let fate tell her that the child ran away from her dad again and somehow tracked her down. That just couldn't be. Could it?

"Hello again," a familiar deep voice rang out from behind the child.

Looking up, her gaze settled on the same face from the other day. "Logan?"

Nodding, he smiled. "Looks like we're neighbors."

She looked from one girl to the other, both hanging at their father's side smiling up at her. "Have you lived here long?"

"About two weeks."

"Two weeks?" How had she not noticed them in two weeks?

"I'd prefer a house with a yard, but not knowing anything about the Houston area, I felt it made more sense to use the corporate housing while I found my footing."

"Sound decision." She glanced down at her watch. "I

really hate to run off, but I overslept and am seriously late. We'll catch up another time. Yes?"

"We're also heading out." He pulled the door closed and quickly turned the lock, the girls now hovering by Leah.

"Can I help you carry something?" Michelle asked sweetly.

"Well," Leah glanced down at all the things precariously balanced in her grip, "maybe my coffee?"

"Okay." She beamed up at her and Leah's heart pretty much melted in place.

Leah had no idea why fate was pushing children on her so hard, but at least these two were cute as a button.

Logan had no idea what he'd done for God to hand him a pretty neighbor who liked his children, but he was most definitely thankful.

"Do you like your work?" Michelle asked their new neighbor.

"Yes, yes I do." Even though Leah had said she was in a hurry, she kept the slower pace with the girls as they all moved down the exterior hallway. "I like helping people and making things a little better for others too."

"Daddy likes his job," Trish volunteered. "Though he said some pretty ugly words when he told my aunt Mary that we were moving to Texas."

"Trish." He did his best to admonish the free flow of information.

"What? I didn't tell her you said it was a pain in the ass."

"Trish." Her sister frowned at her. The kid was only nine years old but had taken on the role of parent almost as much as Logan had. "Daddy told you that you have to be a grown-up to use words like that and only under very serious situations."

"Like when the man who Daddy cut off with his car the

other day shouted out the window for him to—"

"That will be enough, Trish." Mortified, Logan was relieved to notice rather than be judgmental, Leah was biting down on her lips trying not to laugh. "I'm sorry about that. Kids are such sponges."

"No problem," she chuckled. "I know a few adults whose filters could use adjusting."

Okay, so the lady liked kids, had patience with them, and probably him, and a sense of humor. What more could he ask for in a neighbor?

At the bottom of the steps, in one of the first few parking spots, Leah paused, shifting the items balanced in her arms, and reached for her door handle.

"Please." He stretched his hand out and she handed him her briefcase making it easier to yank the door open and drop her purse in the seat, then toss the sweater over onto the passenger seat before straightening and facing him.

"Thanks. A third arm would have come in handy."

"Anytime." He really wanted to say something profound and gripping but standing this close, he noticed for the first time how her smile made her eyes sparkle, and nothing could peel his tongue away from the roof of his mouth.

"Do you want this?" Trish held out the travel mug.

"You bet I do." Leah smiled at the child and accepted the cup, taking a long, noisy, slurpy sip. "Delicious. Thank you."

The way Trish beamed anyone would have thought she'd made the coffee herself.

Maybe it was a mom thing to be so playful with the kids. For someone who said she didn't have children, she did a fabulous job relating to his daughters.

"I'm afraid I really need to get going now." She patted Trish on the head and turned to Logan. "Thanks again for the help."

He shrugged. "It was the least I could do for all the help you've been to me. I'd love it if you'd let me thank you more formally, maybe a nice dinner?"

Her smile no longer reached her eyes as her gaze darted

from him to the girls and back. "Another thank you isn't necessary. Really. It was my pleasure to help and," she held up her cup, "you've already helped me in return."

"Very well." He may not have been out on many dates recently, but he still recognized a polite brush off when he saw it.

"Don't you want to have dinner with us?" Trish asked, her sweet smile replaced by a pouty lower lip.

"Daddy makes really good dinosaur pancakes," Michelle added.

A look of sheer panic flashed in her gaze so briefly he wasn't totally sure if he'd actually seen it or only imagined it.

"I'd like to sometime, but right now I have a very big case and I'm going to be very busy for a little while."

"Then you'll come soon?" Trish's smile returned.

Leah nodded, inching closer to her car. "Soon."

"All right, girls. Leah needs to get to work and so do I. Let's get you off to school."

Sighing, Leah softly mouthed, *Thank you,* then waved at the girls, slipped into her car, and by the time the girls were safely buckled into his practical SUV, Leah was driving off in her stylish Beamer. From his bit of interaction with the woman, the sleek and classic car with just a hint of sexy suited her. Very well.

CHAPTER FIVE

Not since she graduated high school had lingering in bed been something Leah did willingly, but today, she should have just as well made an exception and stayed in bed buried deep under the covers. Not only was she seriously late getting out the door, but the never-ending delays from the morning traffic reminded her why she usually left well before rush hour started. And then, after only an hour behind her desk, a transformer blew in her office neighborhood, sending everybody into black. Once it was clear that the energy company did not expect to fix the problem before end of business day, and her building did not have the generator capacity to supply all the offices in the towering edifice, she had no choice but to pack up her most critical work and head home.

Over the years she'd done her best to set up her home office to work as efficiently as she did downtown, but other than fewer interruptions from staff popping in to ask one question or other, it always seemed like it took twice as many steps to get the same amount of work accomplished.

Scribbling on her notepad, the sound of her doorbell buzzing didn't register the first time, but the longer second buzz had her bouncing out of her seat. No one ever rings her doorbell. Of course, with the work hours she kept, and the time she spent at the ranch, she wasn't usually home that much to actually know how often it rang. Making her way down the hall and across the living room, she glanced at her watch. Six-thirty. How the heck had an eight-hour day gone by and she didn't notice? No wonder her back was aching. She'd have to remember to follow through and buy a better office chair for her apartment. She could work all day and night at her downtown office and her back wouldn't be even a little stiff or sore.

The doorbell buzzed again. "Hold your horses, I'm almost there." She yanked the front door open.

"Pizza. One cheese and one meat lovers." Tall skinny kid who didn't look old enough to drive stood with a huge red vinyl covered box.

"I didn't order pizza."

The kid frowned, looked down at the order, then up at the door, then down again.

"Here." She stretched out her arm and waved her fingers at him. "Let me see that." Someone's teenager might have been pranking the pizza company. The chicken scratch that passed for handwriting was beyond difficult to read. "Here's your problem." She handed him back the paper. "It's for the apartment across the hall."

At that moment, the aforementioned door opened and Logan's head popped out. "Is that for us?"

The kid turned around to face him. "Cheese and meat lovers?"

"Yep." Logan fully opened the door and stepped out. "That's ours."

"Is the pizza here?" First Michelle, then Trish's heads popped out from around either side of their dad.

"It is."

"Hi, Miss Leah." Michelle waved at her enthusiastically. "Teacher told me today that I should call you Miss Leah or Miss your last name. I told her I don't know your last name and she said Miss Leah was okay."

Trish nodded. "It's restable."

Restable? It took Leah a few seconds to figure out the intent, but Michelle beat her to it.

"Respectable," Michelle snapped. "Not restable."

Trish's lower lip did that pouty quiver thing that looked adorable now but Leah doubted it would work in a few more years.

"All right, girls." Logan accepted the two pizzas and handed the kid a tip. "Thank you."

Trish's pouty face transformed instantly as her dad took

possession of their dinner. "Since you're home, you can come eat too."

Leah felt her eyes round like a startled owl. "Uh, well…"

"It's okay." Logan shook his head at her, but before he could say another word, his older daughter stepped fully into the hall.

"We never finish all the pizza. Especially Daddy's one with all the stuff on it. I can set the table." Michelle's expression held such anticipation.

"I can help too." Trish sidled up beside her sister with equal eagerness.

Leah dared look over the two to their dad and his stance reminded her of a defeated client when the jury didn't go their way. She almost felt more sorry for him than for the girls. Her mind ran through all that she needed to do still and quickly decided that disappointing the girls wasn't worth saving a few hours of work later tonight. Besides, she needed to eat at some point, and the look of frustration on Logan's face tugged on her need to make everyone's life a little better.

She bobbed her head. "If it's okay with your dad, I'd love to join you for dinner."

"Absolutely." Logan was as pleased that their new neighbor was joining them as his girls were.

Immediately, Michelle grabbed one of Leah's hands and Trish the other. "Come on."

"Hold on." Leah smiled down at the two children. "I need to grab my keys and lock my door. I'll be right back."

"Come on, girls. We'll wait for Miss Leah inside."

Reluctantly, the girls dragged their feet, following their dad into the apartment.

Michelle stopped, and hands on hips, stared up at her dad. "You need to be on your best behavior."

Funny, he was debating taking these few moments

before Leah arrived to tell his daughters the same thing. He didn't invite people over very often—well, actually, not at all. Not since Deb died.

"This is your first date and you don't want to blow it."

Was his nine-year-old daughter giving him dating advice? "First of all, Miss Miller, this is not a date. This is just a neighbor joining us for pizza."

"Dad." Michelle actually rolled her eyes at him. "She's a woman and she's coming over for dinner. That's a date."

"Miss Leah is a new friend. That's it. Nothing more. Don't go letting your imagination run away with you."

The sound of Leah's door latching shut had them all turning to face the doorway. Diligently, the two girls moved to stand watch for their guest from just inside the doorway. He just hoped there was no discussion of dates in front of Leah.

"Hello," the girls greeted her gleefully.

"Long time no see," Leah teased.

His daughter's laughed, though he wasn't convinced they truly understood the joke.

"Do you want to see our room?" Michelle asked.

"Maybe later. Pizza will get cold." Doing his best to sound calm and casual, Logan was actually battling a swarm of butterflies buzzing about inside him. Setting the pizza on the kitchen island, he opened the boxes, and ripping off the cover, reminded himself of the same thing he'd just told his daughter—this was just a friendly dinner with a neighbor. Too bad those bees in his stomach didn't agree. Though one thing was not up for debate, Leah Baron was a beautiful woman. Exactly the kind to make an awkward man still struggling to master single parenthood, never mind unaccustomed to standing within ten feet of a woman who wasn't a business associate, very nervous.

Without asking, Leah walked behind him into the kitchen. "I'll grab some plates." As if she'd been there many times before, she headed straight for the cabinet where he kept the dishes. "Michelle, why don't you get the silverware, and Trish, the napkins."

Lots of men might be offended that Leah had come into

the kitchen and made herself at home, even instructing his daughters on how to help, but he was perfectly content not to have to worry about entertaining her. More interesting was how both girls nodded politely and did as she'd asked without a single word of argument or debate. It took him a second, but it finally struck him that they were being on extraordinarily good behavior for their dinner guest.

Much to his surprise, there wasn't an awkward or stilted moment at the table. Conversation flowed easily as the girls talked about their day at school, the new friends they were making, a little about their old school, and to his delight, no mention of a dinner invitation being the same thing as a date.

"Do you want a house?" Michelle asked Leah.

Their neighbor nodded. "Some day, yes. But for now, a condo is easier to maintain."

"We want a house." Trish nodded. "Daddy says we have to be patient."

"Come on, girls. Let's clear the table."

Leah pushed to her feet.

"Not you." Logan waved her back. "Guests don't clear the table."

"This one does." She picked up her plate and glass and followed everyone to the kitchen.

With the kitchen all cleaned up, the leftover pizza stored in the fridge, and the dining table cleaned off, guest or no guest, it was time for the girls to get ready for bed. "You know what's next."

Both girls tightened their lips. He could see them getting ready to fuss but also the effort to not fuss in front of Leah. Then Michelle moved to one side of her and Trish to the other. "Will you read us a bedtime story?"

Leah glanced up at him.

"It's okay if Miss Leah reads to us. Right, Daddy?" Trish looked pleadingly at him.

"I don't mind letting someone else read instead of me, but I'm sure Miss Leah has things she needs to do."

"We have a tent in our room." Trish looked up at Leah as if that would be the deciding factor, much the way a pool in the backyard could make or break a real estate deal.

"I'd love to read to you," Leah said.

A few minutes later, the girls were in their pajamas, teeth brushed, and dragging Leah into their room.

"Wow." The woman bobbed her head, looking around. "This is great."

He'd done his best to make the rental a fun place for them. He'd turned a tent into a play fort and put glow in the dark stars on the ceiling. He'd also hung a net in the corner for the menagerie of stuffed animals, but they always wound up on the floor.

"I see lots of horses." Leah picked up two different stuffed ponies as she settled onto the bed beside the girls. "Who likes horses?"

Both girls gleefully shouted, "Me!"

Michelle tucked a midsize pink pony into her side. "Daddy says when we're bigger we can learn to ride real horses."

"Have you ever been on a horse?"

The two shook their heads. Arms crossed, he stood in the doorway watching and listening. The scene gave his heart a kick. He knew the girls missed their mom as much as he did, but no matter how hard he tried, he would never fill his late wife's shoes.

"Well, if your daddy says it's okay, my grandfather has horses and I bet if we visit some day, he'd let you ride them."

"Really?" Both girls squealed.

"Really." Leah smiled. "But it has to be okay with your father."

"Daddy?" They both looked at him pleadingly.

Logan pushed away from the wall and stepped into the room. "Miss Leah and I will discuss it. Now, pick a story."

Of course their choice was a horse story. Leah read it patiently, raising and lowering her voice appropriately at different parts. When it was over, she promised some night she'd read them one of her favorites, then she tucked them in and kissed each on the cheek before he drew in close and did the same. Lights off, he closed the door and sighed.

"They really are sweet."

"Thank you."

"I never have given much thought to how hard it must be for a single parent to raise children. How long has your wife been gone?"

"I'm guessing too long isn't the answer you want."

She shook her head.

"Almost three years. Some days I worry that Trish won't remember her."

"They both will," she said softly.

In the living room, he paused by the door. "Would you like a cup of coffee, tea, a glass of wine—if I can find a bottle?"

Chuckling, she shook her head. "I do have work to do, but thank you for dinner."

Standing, holding the door open, he asked. "Do you really think your grandfather will let the girls ride?"

"Absolutely," she said. "I'll talk to him and get back to you."

"Thank you," he smiled at her. "For everything,"

CHAPTER SIX

orking on this blasted case until almost two this morning, Leah told herself that sleeping in just this one Saturday was not a mortal sin. After the loss of electricity earlier in the week, she'd returned to arriving at work before rush hour traffic and not coming home until late at night. In the case of last night—very late.

A small part of her had considered leaving the office early a night or two and finishing up her work from home in order to knock on Logan's door and let him know that her grandfather and cousin Mitch had indeed agreed to let the girls ride. As a matter of fact, the Governor had gone so far as to suggest the whole family come over for a Sunday afternoon barbecue. While the idea would be fun for her, she knew it would include a truckload of Barons and that might be a bit overwhelming for Logan. It was obvious the man already had his hands full raising two girls on his own, he needed an afternoon with a hundred question-asking relatives like he needed a hole in his head. In the end, working all night, every night had won out. She'd have to slip a note under his door or something.

Pulling the blankets over her shoulders, she rolled over and promised herself five more minutes, maybe ten, when the doorbell rang. Ignoring the buzz, she pulled the covers over her ear. Again the thing sounded. One eye open, she stared across the room, mentally daring the bell to ring again. Ready to snuggle into the bed again, the doorbell sounded for the third time. "Fine," she muttered, throwing the covers off and stomping across the living room. She flung the door open, practically growling, "Hello."

It took a second to realize she needed to look down, not

straight ahead.

"Hello." Trish smiled up at her.

"Good morning."

Michelle came running up beside her sister. "Did you tell her?"

"Michelle?" Logan's voice carried out the open door across the hall.

"No." Trish shook her head. "Not yet."

"Trish? Are you ready?" Logan called out again.

"We're going to the zoo today."

"Isn't that nice." What else could she say? She needed coffee to be clever.

"Girls." A panic-stricken expression washed over Logan's face as he crossed the hall and settled one hand on each child. "What have I told you about bothering Miss Leah?"

"No bother." Her wide yawn most likely belied the statement. "As a matter of fact, I've been meaning to tell you that my grandparents extended an invitation to you and the girls for this Sunday."

"Oh." Something akin to turmoil seemed to flicker in his eyes.

"They're quite looking forward to meeting the girls," she added, to reassure it would not be an imposition.

"Thank you." He nodded, his features more relaxed. "That's very kind—"

"Do you want to come to the zoo with us?" Trish interrupted.

Before she could say a word, Michelle frowned. "You do like the zoo?"

Leah nodded. She did indeed like any zoo, but right now, she was more interested in caffeine.

"Good. Then you'll come." Michelle smiled up at her.

"Well. I haven't had my coffee yet. And I'm still in pajamas."

"We'll wait." The two girls sported matching grins. Irresistible grins.

"I'm sorry." Logan shook his head. "I didn't know they were coming over here." Spinning the girls around, he nudged them toward their own door. "Time to let Miss Leah have her coffee. We can invite her to the zoo another time."

"But Daddy, it's not the same without a grown-up girl." Michelle sounded so forlorn.

"Are you in a hurry?" Leah had no idea she was about to speak until she heard her own words. Good thing she didn't have to go up against cute children attorneys in a courtroom.

The two girls' heads whipped around. "We can wait."

Good, irresistible, smart and determined. One heckuva combination. She didn't want to be in their father's shoes in another ten years. "Give me ten minutes to grab a quick shower and dress. I'll bring my coffee with me."

She'd showered and dressed in record time. Coffee in her favorite travel mug, she hurried out the door. The neighbor's door was open and she rapped on the frame. "Yoo hoo."

"Let's go!" Trish shouted happily.

"You sure about this?" Logan asked from the doorway.

Leah smiled. "It will be fun."

He shrugged and closed and locked the door. "We're off."

It had been years since she'd been to the zoo. Once she'd had a decent amount of coffee in her, she actually began to look forward to the visit. "There are probably a lot of new exhibits since I was last at the zoo."

"When did you last go?" Logan asked from the passenger seat of the car.

Closing one eye, she glanced up, thinking. "Twelve years."

His eyes popped open wide and she had to chuckle. "I told you it was a while."

The eagerness of the girls as they passed through the entrance was not only palpable but beyond contagious. The laughter of gleeful children mixed with the distant roar of animals created a lively soundtrack to the start of their outing.

"Oh, look." Leah pointed to the left at the cotton candy vendor. "Perfect start to the day."

From the way Logan's brows flew up his forehead, she too late realized loading the girls with sugar this early in the day was probably not her best idea, but too late to backtrack now. A few minutes later, sticky fingers and all, the four of them laughed and joked at the nearby lounging sea lions, who seemed to be talking directly to them, wanting the cotton candy they held.

From there, they hurried over to the wildlife carousel. Rather than colorful ponies, the massive ride boasted lions, and giraffes, and hippos, along with other jungle animals painted in bright and cheery colors that would improve the sourest of dispositions.

"Can we ride this, Daddy?" Michelle practically bounced in place.

"Sure." He ruffled the top of her hair. "We're here to have fun."

Helping Trish onto the bright red parrot, Leah's cheeks actually hurt from smiling so much. Anyone would have thought the little kid was actually riding a colorful bird ready to soar over the Houston skies. The funnier thing, Leah felt as though maybe, just maybe, as laughter and joy filled the air, like Mary Poppins and the magic carpet bag, anything today was possible.

When Logan had suggested he and the girls go to the zoo this weekend, including Leah had not been part of his plan. Now, he couldn't imagine this day without her.

As they approached the giraffe exhibit, where the long-necked giants gracefully nibbled at leaves, Michelle and Trish's eyes widened with excitement.

"Daddy, look! Giraffes!" Michelle exclaimed, tugging at Logan's hand. "Those people are feeding the giraffes. I want to feed the giraffes."

Without thinking, he looked over to Leah to silently ask if that was a good or bad idea. As absurd as it was to be asking a single woman, a near stranger, if the activity was inappropriate for small children, it was even more absurd that she seemed to understand his expression and shrugged an answer.

Still slightly unsure, he was relieved to see a multitude of kids even smaller than Trish lined up to feed the long-necked animals. When their turn came, each adult stood behind a child.

Trish stiffened unexpectedly. "That's a big head."

From the ground, the animals looked majestic and tall, but not till they were on the feeding platform did it become obvious how massive the animals really were. At two feet, a giraffe's head was almost half as long as Trish was tall. His little girl stepped back until she bumped into Leah.

"What's the matter, Trish?"

Perfectly still, his little girl didn't say a word.

"Trish?" Logan asked. "What's the matter, honey?"

"It's big." She seemed fixated on the giraffe staring at her.

"I think he's waiting for you to feed him?" Leah encouraged her. "See, like this." Leah stretched out her hand holding a lettuce leaf. A long, thick, black tongue slipped out between the animal's lips and the next thing they knew, the leaf was gone and the giraffe was munching away.

To his delight, rather than remain frightened, Trish giggled.

"Our turn." Michelle grabbed the lettuce piece and held it out to the waiting animal. Just as the other one had done, the long tongue came out and then the leaf was gone. "Can we do that again?"

Logan nodded. "They gave us each three leaves of lettuce."

"Do you want to try?" Leah leaned over Trish's shoulder and spoke softly near her ear.

It took her a moment, but she finally nodded and reached for the proffered lettuce leaf. Another moment and the giraffe had stuck out his tongue and as Trish leaned back and away, the giraffe inched closer until he snatched the leaf and straightened, munching away.

Trish spun around and laughed heartily. "One more time?"

"Of course," Leah answered, handing her the leaf.

From the giraffe feeding platform to the elephants to the train ride and back to the reflection pool, Trish laughed and giggled with her sister and couldn't stop talking about feeding the giraffes and how happy they were to have Leah there with them. Every five minutes they were calling Leah over to look at one animal or another. With his permission, she'd bought them a few souvenirs along the way. Strolling side by side toward the reflection pool, Logan and Leah watched the girls skipping just ahead of them.

"You know," Logan chuckled at his girls bopping along, "I think you may be their favorite part of this day."

"Nonsense." She shook her head.

Reaching the pool a minute behind the girls, as they'd done all day, each adult stood behind a child. It reminded him of something a friend had said many years ago about raising three children instead of two: *You're always one arm of one parent short*. One adult per child, he realized now that advice made perfect sense.

"It's beautiful." Michelle stared out at the shimmering pool with fountains under a canopy of mature live oak trees. "Like you," she whispered.

Chuckling, Logan shrugged. "I don't think she means me."

The look of disbelief on Leah's face was a surprise. Did she really not know she was beautiful?

"Like a princess," Trish added. Only this time, the little girl looked over her shoulder at Leah. "You're more beautiful than a princess." A frown fell over her expression. "Can you make me pretty like you?"

"Oh, honey." Leah squatted down to be eye level with his youngest child. "You already are beautiful." Her finger ran through the long curls gathered into a ponytail. "I would kill to have golden curls like this."

"Really?" Trish touched the ends of her own hair.

"Really. And you and Michelle have such pretty eyes."

Michelle nodded and smiled brightly. "Daddy says we

have Mommy's eyes."

"Well, your mommy must have been very beautiful to have two little girls like you who are as pretty on the inside as you are on the outside."

The two girls smiled and turned back, a look of complete contentment on their faces. As far as he was concerned, they were absolutely correct. Leah was very pretty, but what she'd said about his girls was as true for her. She was as pretty on the inside as she was on the outside.

CHAPTER SEVEN

Whenever her day job gave her a moment's pause, Leah's mind rushed back to the Saturday at the zoo. Even as a kid she was pretty sure she hadn't enjoyed the zoo as much as she did seeing it through the eyes of Logan's daughters. Sitting at her home desk between the lamp and her file holder was the stuffed giraffe Trish had insisted on giving her.

Just remembering how she picked it out all by herself and then pulled a curled up dollar bill from her pocket and proudly handed it over to the sales clerk, made Leah beam. The sales clerk graciously accepted the dollar from Trish, thanked her, then subtly looked to Logan who just as discreetly handed the man his credit card for the difference. When Trish turned around and gifted it to Leah, she almost cried. No wonder parents would move heaven and earth to make their children happy.

She'd never had so much respect and appreciation for her parents love and sacrifices as she did after this past weekend. Granted, being born a Baron, there was rarely an issue of financial sacrifice, but that didn't diminish the constant patience and quality time her parents shared even when there were other things pressing. Those efforts were worth their weight in gold. She also appreciated more why her grandfather was so anxious for great-grandchildren. While Leah had often thought of children as loud and disruptive nuisances, she now had to acknowledge that some kids were just plain precious. Trish and Michelle fell into the latter category.

Heading to the kitchen for a refill of her hot tea, she'd just about hit the kitchen when a repetitive rap on the front door sounded. She was beginning to get used to regular visits from her neighbors. Where once upon a time she'd have questioned who the heck was knocking, now she was pretty sure she knew who was at the door. Swinging it open, she smiled, looking down. "Hello."

"Daddy needs help," Trish spurted out, grabbing her by the hand and dragging her across the hall. "Michelle can't find the Band-Aids."

"Band-Aids?" Her mind began to spin. Debating stopping the child from tugging her away from her own apartment and rushing back for a first aid kit, she opted to find out what the situation was. After all, it could be something as simple as a paper cut or hang nail.

Crossing the threshold of Logan's apartment, she could hear water running from the direction of the kitchen, but the most startling thing was the droplets of blood on the floor. Panic threatened to overwhelm her. Years of courtroom training helped her shove the fear for the worst out of the way. "Logan?"

"Leah? I told the girls not to bother you."

Letting go of Trish's hand, she hurried in the direction of the kitchen and Logan's voice. "What happened?"

His hand under the sink, he had a kitchen towel spotted with blood to one side. "We had a little accident."

"We?" She looked down at Trish. "Where's Michelle?"

"She's in the bathroom looking for Band-Aids." He paused a moment. "Can you get me a clean dish towel from the drawer by the stove?"

Scanning the cabinets, she pulled open the top drawer beside the oven and grabbed a dark blue towel. Depending on what was going on, she didn't want a white towel that might look like a prop from a true crime drama.

The minute she sidled up beside him, she saw the problem. "How did you do that?"

He sighed, lowering his voice. "Rinsing out a glass by hand, the thing simply snapped and cut across my knuckles. I tried to put pressure and get to the bathroom where the first aid things are stored, but it was too much of a mess and the look on Trish's face had me hurrying back to the sink."

"Yeah, well, this way you'll just bleed out eventually." Shaking her head, she reached for his hand. "Do you know if there's any glass in the cuts?"

"I don't think so. The glass appears to be a clean snap."

In the other side of the sink was the broken glass. Lifting it carefully, she examined the evidence. It did appear to have been a clean break with no shards, but with glass one never knew. "Okay. We've got to stop the bleeding." She grabbed several paper towels, folded them, and pressed them against his cut. Wincing when she saw the white of his knuckles, she whispered to him, "This may need stitches."

He bobbed his head. "I thought the same." Then his gaze darted to where his daughters stood at the kitchen doorway just watching.

Noticing the girls, Leah did what any good litigator would do. Bluff. "Well, this isn't so bad," she said quite loudly. "Girls, why don't you find something Daddy might like to watch on television and as soon as I get him cleaned up we'll all watch a nice movie?"

Relief immediately taking over their faces, they turned and ran to the living room.

"Thanks. I didn't know quite how to do this without making the place look like a crime scene."

All she did was nod, press the paper towels against the cut, then wrap the dish towel tightly around it. "Raise your hand up. We have to slow the bleeding. I'll keep putting pressure on it. Then when the flow slows, I can see if you're going to need to get stitches or not."

"If I can avoid it, that would be my preference. I don't want to take the girls to the hospital."

"Well, you have about twenty-four hours to decide. After that they can't do stitches even if you need them."

With blood all over the paper towels and sink, she did her best to wipe up so the girls wouldn't be frightened, but from her vantage, this was not looking so good.

★

As much as he enjoyed Leah's company, Logan was never as happy to see her cross his threshold as he was tonight. Somehow he would have figured it all out, but having a helper made all the difference in the world. Having a pretty helper was just the cherry on top. He wasn't even going to mention the upside of having said pretty woman holding his hand. Though a lot of folks would debate squeezing pressure onto sliced knuckles wasn't quite the same as holding hands, he was willing to ignore that small tidbit.

Standing like the Statue of Liberty with has hand up the air, he felt like an idiot. But he did understand Leah's logic. And he had to admit, the hand throbbed less when he kept it elevated. Like a puppy following after his new master, he followed Leah into the living room.

"Sit." She waved at the sofa.

"Yes, sir. Uh, ma'am."

Thankfully, she chuckled at him. "Military background?"

He shook his head. "No, but I loved the show *JAG* as a kid. Does that count?"

She laughed even harder. "We'll see."

As soon as he was comfortably seated, Leah grabbed some nearby throw pillows and piled them at his side. "Girls, could one of you please bring me the pillows from your dad's bed?"

The two ran off as if they'd been told there was a pot of gold at the end of the hall.

"More pillows?" He had no idea what she was thinking.

"I want your arm higher but I don't want you having to hold it up or you'll get really tired really soon."

Each carrying a pillow, the girls ran back into the room.

Leah puffed, propped, and shifted the pillows until his arm was sticking up in the air, but well supported. He had to admit, he was indeed fairly comfortable, and thankfully, the throbbing was down to a low buzz.

"I'm hungry," Trish uttered very close to a whine.

Blowing out a sigh, he rolled his eyes. So distracted with slicing his hand open, he forgot that he hadn't yet fixed supper. He leaned slightly forward when Leah placed a hand on his shoulder, holding him in place.

"Where do you think you're going?"

"To fix dinner."

She shook her head. "Not happening." Standing up, she dropped her hands on her hips. "What were you going to make?"

"Meatloaf. But it's getting late, there's really not enough time before bedtime to cook a dinner." Stupid hand. "Girls, what do you say to peanut butter and jelly sandwiches for dinner?"

Some days he would bet his life savings that these two were actually twins born a few years apart. Not one but both scrunched their noses in disapproval.

"With potato chips?"

The two looked at each other and for a moment he thought he was going to win this battle easily, but in the next moment the noses scrunched up again and the heads shook from side to side.

"Do you have cold cuts?" Leah asked softly, her back to the girls.

He nodded.

"Bologna?" she asked.

"I think so."

Slapping her hands together and rubbing them vigorously, Leah turned to face the girls. "How about a nice fried bologna sandwich?"

The frown of disapproval shifted to a confused wrinkled brow.

"Trust me," she reached for the girls, nudging them toward the kitchen, "you're going to love it."

Thank heaven she was right. Eating in the living room so that he wouldn't have to move his arm, they settled in for the rest of the movie. To his relief, the sandwiches were a big hit. At bedtime, Leah wouldn't let him move yet, and the girls were more than happy to let her run them through the bedtime routine. When Leah came out of the room and closed the door behind her, Logan didn't know if he was relieved that things went smoothly, or a little sad that his girls didn't need him.

"All right. Time to check that hand."

"Good. My fingers have been asleep for almost an hour."

"What?" Her eyes rounded wide and her jaw dropped just enough for him to see the tip of her tongue through her teeth.

"Kidding. But it has fallen asleep." He lowered the arm and wiggled his fingers. At least most of the sting and throb was gone.

Taking hold of his hand, Leah carefully unwrapped it, then gently ran her fingers along the exposed skin.

Logan actually had to remind himself he was injured and she was merely being neighborly, but the truth was her touch was sending fiery sensations up his arm.

"I don't think there's any glass, so that's good. It also seems to have stopped bleeding, but I'm afraid if you move your fingers too much the cut will open again. Do you have any butterfly Band-Aids?"

"I don't even know what that is."

"Bandage tape?"

He nodded and pushed to his feet, but before taking a step, he turned to her. "May I move now?"

Chuckling, she nodded. A few minutes later she'd criss-crossed the tape over the cuts and bobbed her head with satisfaction. "I think you're going to be good to go, but you may want to see a doctor in case they think you need stitches."

"Will do. I appreciate the save."

"That's what neighbors are for."

"Please let me thank you properly." She blinked twice and her shoulders stiffened, signaling that he probably could have phrased that differently. "May I take you out to a proper dinner? Somewhere that doesn't fry bologna?"

That, thankfully, made her laugh.

"It's the least I can do," he added.

It took her another moment to nod, then slowly smile.

Fortunately, his hand was now wrapped up again and propped on that same dumb pillow because he would have looked totally ridiculous doing a fist pump when she agreed to an adult dinner with him.

CHAPTER EIGHT

Hair wrapped in a towel, still in her bathrobe, Leah stared into her closet. Nothing in the informal invitation to dinner tonight implied what type of restaurant Logan had in mind. Doesn't serve fried bologna sandwiches covered an awful lot of territory. In the end, she grabbed a simple black sleeveless dress. A strand of pearls would dress it up if he took her somewhere elegant, and a pair of sandals would dress it down if they wound up at a casual neighborhood spot.

The way she debated pulling her hair back, leaving it down, maybe even flipping it up in a sloppy bun, anyone would think she'd never been on a first date before. Hair brush in hand, she stopped mid-stroke. Perhaps even looking at this as a date was a mistake. After all, all he said was a thank you dinner. A way of showing his appreciation for her interaction with his daughters.

That little revelation cemented in her mind to keep everything very casual. Flat sandals, hair down, and her makeup the way she would go to work. Somehow, having decided on this took away some of the raw edges of her nerves.

The doorbell sounded and she looked down at her watch. Why would he show up an hour early? Tightening the belt on her robe, she hurried to the front door and swung it open.

Held up in the air, two large brown bags covered her visitor's face. Dropping them down to arm height, her sister Claire pushed into the room. "Was in the neighborhood and remembered that delicious Chinese restaurant around the corner. Since I'm starving, I figured you must be too."

Her sister was in the kitchen emptying bags before Leah could utter a word. "I hope you still like the Crab Rangoon. I got a double order."

"In that case, I hope you're very hungry."

The unexpected response had her sister looking up from the bags. "Why are you ready for bed at this early hour?"

Once again, she nervously retied the belt on her robe. "Not ready for bed, getting ready to go out to dinner."

Her sister's eyes rounded. "You mean a date?"

"Don't look so surprised." Again, she tighten the belt. "But as it turns out, it's not a real date."

"So it's a fake date?" Her sister continued emptying food containers from the bags.

"Did you think otherwise?" There had to be at least ten containers of food on the counter so far.

Claire waved off her sister's comment. "There's no crime against being hungry, and stop evading the question. This isn't your courtroom. Spill. I want all the juicy details."

"Sorry to disappoint you." Leah snatched a wonton and turned away. "I'm just joining a neighbor for a bite to eat."

"Wait." Claire turned and ran after her sister. "Are we talking the neighbor you mentioned with the little girl who tried to buy you?"

Wishing she hadn't said anything, Leah nodded and continued into her room, whipping the towel off her head. "That's right. Nothing more than a thank you for not reporting into Social Services." She chuckled in an effort to play down the entire situation. Not that there was anything to play down. After all, she had just decided herself that it wasn't really a date.

Claire scanned the top of her bed, pausing over the black dress, then shifted her gaze to the vanity where Leah had laid out her pearls. "So help me if you have chosen black strappy stiletto heels to go with this, there is no way in heck I am going to believe this is nothing more than a casual dinner between neighbors."

Spinning around, Leah stuck her tongue out at her sister and held out the ordinary black sandals she'd chosen. "I'm telling you, it's just dinner."

"Too bad." Claire plopped down on the bed, crossing her legs in a yoga position. "Only seems fair that one of us should have a decent love life."

Pulling out the hair dryer, Leah paused to face her sister. "This explains all the Chinese food. What happened?"

Claire pulled a pillow against her chest, and hugging it, shrugged. "Same old same old. I overheard David chatting with his friend before he noticed me approaching. He was patting himself on the back for landing such a good catch."

"Uh-oh." Leah looked at the mirror to better see Claire behind her. Money could be a blessing, but it was also one of the biggest pitfalls of being a member of the Baron family. "I'm guessing not in a *what a great gal* sort of way but a *what a nice bank account* way."

With her finger on the tip of her nose, Claire nodded. "Give the girl a prize."

Having people target you for your money was one of the most unsettling experiences a girl, or even guy, could have to deal with. It happened all too often in the Baron family. "I'm really sorry, sweetie." Her hair dry, she set down the dryer and stood to give her sister a hug.

Holding on tightly before letting go and sitting back, Claire shrugged again. "At least this time we didn't date long enough for me to really care about losing him, it's just so frustrating."

Boy, did she know what her sister meant.

"I'll get some food while you finish dressing." Claire popped up from the bed, already her expression a bit brighter. Sometimes all a woman needed was a sister to commiserate with.

Dressed and ready to go, she'd entered the living room to find her sister at the island eating out of a white container. "Are you going to eat all of this?"

Fork in hand, Claire grinned up at her. "Maybe." At that the door bell rang and Claire lifted her gaze to the clock over the fridge. "Ooh, and he's early, must be excited." That sappy *I know something you don't* grin took over again.

Swinging the door open, Leah plastered on a friendly but not too friendly smile. "You're early."

"We have a little problem." Logan stood stiffly on the other side of the door.

"Oh." Her first thought ran to something was wrong with one of the girls.

"My babysitter just canceled. One of my co-workers recommended her and frankly, I don't have any back-ups."

Leah frowned. Babysitters weren't something she had a long list of.

A throat cleared from the kitchen, followed quickly by Claire standing behind her, grinning up at all six-foot-two, dark hair, and blue-eyed Logan, her older sister stuck her hand out. "Claire Baron, at your services."

"Well, that turned out much better than I could have hoped for. I thought for sure we were going to have to order pizza or wait for another day." Logan pulled out of the parking space. "I hate to admit it, but today was rather harried at work. First day for a new batch of transferees from California, and if anything could go wrong, it did. Three people showed up, who we weren't told were coming, so their offices weren't ready. I had no idea I had so many resourceful people working with me."

"That's good."

"The resourceful part, yes, the not having your VP of operations office ready, not so much."

"Ouch." She actually looked as pained as he'd felt most of the afternoon. Of all his bosses, this particular one was the least accommodating. "Thankfully, the senior VP of finance was happy to give up his corner office to the operations grump in order to keep the peace."

"Well, I suppose that's a good thing."

"Absolutely." Stopping for a red light, he turned to face her. "I made reservations at the Woodfire. I hope that's okay."

"It's one of my favorites."

"I've heard great things about it, and almost called to see if you were vegetarian or vegan or something like that, but then I remembered you made and ate bologna sandwiches so figured I was all set."

"More than all set. My grandparents own a working cattle ranch. It's pretty much sacrilegious to be a vegetarian."

He couldn't help but laugh, and laugh loudly. "I can see where that might not sit well with your grandparents."

"Agreed."

"I'm so glad that your sister likes kids."

"Well," she chuckled, "I don't know if I'd go that far, but at least she doesn't dislike them."

"Really? She seemed to get right in on their level. The girls didn't mind staying with her at all."

"Maybe it's got something to do with her being a veterinarian. Animals love her, looks like kids might too."

"And here we are." He turned into the tiny parking lot and frowned at all the cars. He'd made the reservation a couple of days ago even though his coworker who recommended it warned him it might be hard. Looking at the packed parking lot, he understood why.

Forced to park around back, he hurried around the car and opened the door for Leah. Tempted to take hold of her hand, he settled for putting his hands safely in his pockets until it was time to open the restaurant door.

"Do you have a reservation?" the blonde who didn't look old enough to vote smiled up at him.

"Yes. Logan Miller. Seven-fifteen."

The young lady looked down at a screen and after a few moments frowned, finally glancing back up. "I'm sorry. I don't see it. Logan?"

"Miller. I called a couple of days ago. Spoke to a gentleman."

"Oh, dear. You're down for tomorrow night."

That wasn't what he wanted to hear. "I see. Any chance you have a corner for two tonight?"

The frown on the young girl's face deepened. "I'm sorry."

"Something wrong, Jamie?" An older gentleman in a tie and jacket appeared behind the young girl. She quickly explained as he perused the screen. "I'm terribly sorry, but I'm afraid we don't have..." the man's gaze shifted from Logan to Leah. "Oh, Ms. Baron. I didn't realize you were looking for a table."

"Hi, Jeremy. So you finally put your daughter to work?" Leah smiled up at him.

"Her sister left for law school. It was time." He grabbed two menus and taking a step back, looked at Logan. "If you'll follow me, please."

Leah did say she loved the place, but he didn't expect the manager to know her well enough to find them a table. The gentleman chatted briefly with Leah, asking after her parents, grandparents, and siblings. The conversation only lasted a few moments, but long enough for him to wonder just how often did these people eat here?

"Sorry about that." Leah slipped her napkin onto her lap. "This really is a nice place to eat."

"The manager seems like a nice guy."

"Actually," she reached for her water glass, "he's the owner. He and his wife started this place ages ago. My grandfather discovered it long before it was so popular."

"Miss Baron." A waiter stopped at their table. "So nice to see you again. It's been a while."

"Thank you, Oscar."

"Will you be having your chocolate martini to start?"

"Thank you. That would be lovely."

"And you, sir?" The waiter turned to face him.

His mind circling around not only did the waiter know Leah, but she knew the waiter as well, that he had no idea what the man had asked. "Excuse me?"

"Would you like a drink?"

"Oh. Yes. I'll have a martini please. No chocolate."

"Coming right up." The waiter turned on his heel.

Logan had never had such VIP treatment in a restaurant before. All that his mind could focus on was, just who the heck was his neighbor?

CHAPTER NINE

"Chocolate Martini is like dessert before dinner. You don't know what you're missing." Leah smiled up at him.

Logan was sure he was definitely missing something. "Just how often do you come here for dinner?"

"Actually, I haven't been here in at least a year. But this is a favorite haunt for a lot of my family. And I have a really big family."

He supposed that could explain it, but something just wasn't connecting. "Remind me how many siblings you have?"

"Well, there are only five of us and a platoon's worth of cousins, making an awful lot of Barons running around the Houston area."

"That's right. Now I remember."

"Uncle Bradley is the one who had seven kids with four wives. My uncle Doug had four children with two wives, but his first wife passed away."

"I gather not so with Uncle Bradley?"

Rolling her eyes, she shook her head. "Not only did he divorce all three wives, or more accurately they divorced him, but he didn't bother to wait for his first wife to divorce him before finding his second wife. If you know what I mean."

"I think I do." Every family had their skeletons or black sheep. Looked like Uncle Bradley was the lucky winner in the Baron family.

Another waiter appeared with their drinks. "Your martini, Miss Baron. The way you like it, light on vodka with extra cream."

"Thank you, Tim."

"Sir." The waiter slid the ordinary martini in front of him. "Oscar will be back momentarily to take your order."

"Thank you," Logan spoke up, while Leah held her glass up to him.

"Cheers."

"Cheers," he repeated. "Thank you for all you've done to help me out."

Her grin blossomed. "It's been my pleasure."

"I freely admit, this whole move, getting used to a new state, new schools, new office, heck, even maneuvering a new grocery store has all been more challenging than I anticipated."

"I can't imagine. I've lived in Houston my whole life. I have my favorite everything from specialty cheese shop to a mom-and-pop gift store. Starting over with kids has to be doubly tough."

Since his wife passed, everything was doubly tough. His mind, with a will of its own, began wandering down memory lane uninvited.

"Are you okay?" Her fingers barely grazed the top of his hand to capture his attention and yet the unexpected spark captured way more than his attention.

"Yes. Sorry. I've mostly gotten used to it being just the girls and me, but every so often memories sneak up on me."

"It has to be hard."

"Actually, my late wife was a great mother. She believed in training a child in the way they should go."

"Book of Proverbs." She smiled.

"That's right. Bedtime is crazy easy because the girls are so used to bedtime comes at seven p.m. and wake up time isn't until seven a.m. It was tough as infants, but Deb pulled it off. They're really great girls."

"Trust me, compared to some kids I've met, your girls are beyond great.

"Thank you." Her heartfelt complement made him smile. It would have made Deb smile too. She always grinned like a fool when anyone complimented the girls.

"Honestly, it had never occurred to me that kids could

be so pleasant to spend time with. Or when you've had a tough day, or week, and would really love to break some idiot's neck, that kids might do or say something that totally makes your day. Like telling you that you remind them of a princess."

He couldn't argue with her there. So many days when life weighed heavily on his shoulders, the sweet smiles and encouraging words from his children had lifted him up again.

"Ready for dessert?" Oscar appeared out of nowhere.

"Actually, yes." Logan looked to her. "Did you leave room?"

"You know I did." Leah grinned up at Oscar.

"Crème brulee?" Oscar asked confidently.

"Absolutely." She leaned forward and touched his hand again. "If you like crème brulee at all, you'll love this."

"Two crème brulees it is." He took a sip of water and debated how to ask what he was thinking. "I, uh, have a question."

"Shoot." Leah dabbed at the corners of her mouth with her napkin before setting it back on her lap.

"If you haven't been here in a year, how come so many waiters still know you by name and know your favorite food and drink? I mean, I used to have a favorite restaurant. Our family went maybe once a month, and I don't think anyone knew my name."

She blew out a deep sigh, stared into the top of her water glass, and then lifted her gaze to meet his. "What do you know about me?"

"Besides that you're a lawyer, my neighbor, single, and like my kids?"

She nodded.

"That's about it."

"Does the name Baron mean anything to you?"

That almost sounded like a trick question. "European royalty?" Oh, lord, she can't be a duchess or something incognito—could she?

"Not exactly. What about the name Mitchell Baron?"

He knew he was staring, but the name didn't mean a thing to him.

"United States Senator Mitchell Baron."

"Sorry." He shook his head. "I don't even know all the senators from my home state. Politics and I are only on a first name basis on election day. And that's just barely. One of your brothers?"

"Cousin. And my grandfather is former Governor James Baron."

Now the picture was becoming more clear. Political pull. Every business owner wanted to make nice with a powerful politician. All he wanted was to make nice with the non-politician family member. What he needed to figure out, was just how nice did he want things to go?

Even though the Woodfire was one of Leah's favorite restaurants, tonight the food was especially delicious. Though she suspected it had more to do with the company than the person in the kitchen.

"You were not exaggerating." Logan took the last bite of his dessert. "This is magnificent."

"Now you know why my whole family loves the food here."

"Makes sense. I suspect this place is going to become one of my favorites too."

The entire dinner had been wonderful, but her heart almost cracked open when he spoke of his wife. Her mind kept circling back to her cousin Mitch when he lost his wife, Abbie. His loss was palpable every time he walked into a room. With Logan, most of the time she didn't sense that pain, until this dinner. Her respect for him as a single parent just inched up the yardstick a few notches.

Once he'd paid the bill, they made their way to the front of the restaurant. His hand briefly on the small of her back, directing her toward the front, left her warmed from the inside out when he pulled it away to open the door.

"Maybe we can check out a few more of your favorite restaurants?" he asked softly.

"Or find new ones?" she replied, holding back a wide smile. Not till he'd suggested going out again did she realize just how much she actually wanted to do just that.

The chit-chat in the car was pleasant, simple, and had her smiling a lot. They avoided the elephants in the room, so to speak—his wife and her family name. And that was just fine with her. By the time they reached his door at the top of the stairs, she was wishing they had a little more time.

Logan unlocked the door and she could see the anticipation on his face. If he'd been worried about the girls during dinner, she'd missed it, but now she could see that he wasn't totally sure what he'd find, and then she saw the utter relief to find Claire watching television and the room pretty much the way they left it. "How did it go?"

"Easy peasy. Your girls follow rules, listen, and honestly, I think I need a babysitter more than they did."

That made everyone in the room laugh. Leah really did love her big sister. She hoped that Michelle and Trish grew up to be even half as close as she and Claire were.

"All right." Claire jumped to her feet. "Hate to baby-sit and run, but it's late and I have to be up bright and early in the morning."

"You okay to drive?" Leah hadn't thought about Claire's long drive home.

"Of course I'm okay, but if you want to offer your sofa for the night, I won't object." Her sister flashed a toothy grin at her.

"It's all yours."

"Great, then I'm going to head out. You two enjoy the rest of your evening. I'll leave the light on for you."

"No, you won't." Leah shook her head. Her sister was making too many assumptions. "I'm coming with you." She turned to face Logan. "Thank you again for a very delicious dinner."

"My pleasure, but thank you. After all, that was the whole point."

She bobbed her head and led the way out the front door, crossed the hall, and unlocked her own door.

They'd barely closed the door behind him when Claire practically bounced in place. "I want to hear it all. Where'd you go? What did you eat? What did you talk about? Did he kiss you? Are you going out on another date? Spill."

"Good grief. Sure you don't want to know his blood type?"

"If you want to share, why not."

Shaking her head, Leah rolled her eyes. "We went to Woodfire."

"Ooh. Good choice."

"I had what I always have. We talked about a lot, including his late wife, of course he didn't kiss me, and it wasn't a date."

A deep-set frown settled between Claire's brows. "Seriously?"

She nodded.

Claire collapsed on the sofa and stared up at her kid sister. "Okay. If you don't want him, can I have him?"

"Of course not." That came out a bit more forcibly than she'd wanted.

"Aha!" Her sister sprang up again. "You like him." The last three words came out more like an accusation than a statement.

"Of course I like him. He's a nice person. A good father. But that doesn't make it a date. Besides," she sat on the other end of the sofa, "I think he's still grieving his wife."

"Grieving?" Claire blew out a slow hiss and sat back down. "He's not divorced?"

Leah shook her head. "Nope."

"Well," Claire grabbed a sofa throw pillow, "Mitch fell in love again."

"Yes, but no one is talking about falling in love here. We're not even dating."

"I hate to break this to you, Sis. But if an invitation to dine at Woodfire isn't a date, I don't know what is."

Leah tugged the throw pillow out of her sister's arms. "I don't know." And for the first time in a long time, she really didn't have a clue what she really felt or what she really wanted. Logan, so far, had proved to be a really nice and thoughtful guy. A part of her thought her infatuation might be more with the girls than the father. But she'd be lying if she said after gently touching his hand to get his attention that pulling her hand away hadn't taken a conscious effort. What she'd really wanted to do was wrap his hand in hers and hang on for the rest of the night. So, where exactly did all this leave her?

CHAPTER TEN

"You're starting to make these early mornings a habit." Leah's grandmother looked up from her spot at the end of the dining table.

"Today is the day that my neighbor is bringing his daughters to ride the horses." Leah stood at the buffet serving herself breakfast. Truth was that Logan and the girls weren't arriving until after lunch, but she was so nervous and excited about how the girls would react with real horses, that she just couldn't sleep. Somewhere around six o'clock she gave up, came down to the kitchen to make herself a cup of coffee, then went upstairs to shower and dress. Here she was, at seven-thirty in the morning, the first of her generation to hit the dining room.

"I would have expected you to come with them this afternoon." Grams took a sip of her coffee.

"Normally, I probably would have, but last night a bunch of us got together for dinner not far from the ranch and it just made more sense to come here than to go home and drive back."

"I, for one, think it is going to be lots of fun having children here." Very likely one of the only men left in the state of Texas who still read a paper newspaper, the Governor set his down on the table next to him. "Remind me how old they are again?"

"Seven and nine."

"Oh, what fun ages," her grandmother exclaimed. "Perfect for learning to ride horses. I know we started most of you a lot younger, but seven and nine is not too late."

"Good morning." Her brother Devlin came into the dining room with her cousin Porter in tow. "Why is it my bed is never as comfortable at my place as it is here?"

"Love." Their grandmother beamed at them.

"You'd know that if you took the time to make your relationship with Emily official." In contrast to his wife's broad smile, the Governor was in full Marine mode, dressing down his troops.

"Governor, I keep telling you. We're just friends. Emily is nice, really she is."

"Pretty too." Porter shrugged when Devlin mouthed silently to him *you're not helping*.

"Friendship is the best foundation for a long marriage," her grandmother sweetly tossed out.

Leah had to struggle to bite back a laugh. Poor Devlin was always getting grief over his friendship with Emily. For a long time, even Leah thought there was something going on, but the more she got to know Emily, the more she realized, like Jack used to be for Eve, Emily was just a friendly plus-one, and visa versa for when she needed a stand-in.

"Marriage? Who's getting married?" Her brother Cooper waltzed into the dining room.

"According to Grams and the Governor, Devlin and Emily." Porter slathered jam on his toast.

"What?" Cooper's jaw dropped, and his eyes practically fell out of his head. "But I thought…"

Hands up in the air, Devlin shook his head. "I am not marrying Emily. I do not love Emily. Emily is a wonderful friend. And yes, she is extremely pretty, but trust me we are just friends."

Leah came within inches of teasing her brother by saying *I think he doth protest too much*, but she could see the steam almost coming out of his ears and figured the poor guy had been tortured enough by their grandparents. "What does everyone have planned for the day?"

"As little as possible." Cooper spoke up first. "If I have to deal with one more unreliable subcontractor, I'm moving to Tahiti."

"That bad?" Devlin asked.

"It's like this week they all got together and decided

let's make Cooper's life hell. I pretty much have it all straightened out, but two days of solid nothing is exactly what the doctor ordered."

"Sounds good." Devlin nodded. "I've got a dinner with some investors tonight. At least I know we'll have a nice dinner."

"Where are you going to eat?" Porter took another bite of his French toast.

How Leah envied his metabolism. Since childhood, Porter seemed to have two hollow legs. All Leah had to do was smell food and she could feel the pounds coming on.

"Woodfire. Can always count on Jeremy for a good meal."

"Absolutely," Leah agreed. "Had dinner there last week for the first time in forever. Never disappoints. And I love those chocolate martinis."

"I don't know how you drink that. It's like a chocolate milkshake with dinner." Devlin made an ugly face.

"Exactly." Leah grinned widely.

"And whom did you have dinner with, dear?"

Open mouth, insert foot. Leah shouldn't have said a word. Her grandparents would latch on to dinner with Logan and the girls coming with him today to ride horses like a lantern hanging in the North Church announcing, instead of the British, a wedding is coming. "Nothing special. Just dinner with a friend."

"A friend?" The Governor stared at her a tad too intently.

"Hate to eat and run." Devlin pushed to his feet. "Just remembered I have to pick something up for one of my clients. If you have a minute, Sis, I could use a little female advice."

"Sure." Leah happily jumped to her feet before her grandfather could dig in further to her dinner the other night.

In the hall, Devlin leaned in, gave her a kiss on the cheek and whispered, "I got nothing, but you owe me for the save."

Throwing her arms around his neck, she gave him a big

kiss on the cheek. "Have I mentioned you're the best brother ever?"

"Not enough." He laughed and headed out the front door. "I have to go somewhere, but I'll be back to meet this man and his daughters."

Sometimes saying nothing was best, so she settled for a nod.

Her grandfather, though he didn't know it, was right about one thing: she was way too nervous and excited about this afternoon's visit. She really, really, *really* wanted Logan and his girls to like her family. It shouldn't matter, but like it or not, it did. Somehow between now and when they arrived, she was going to have to get a handle on what the heck was going on.

"Are we there yet?" Every few minutes either Michelle or Trish asked the same question.

If Logan had ever considered a family road trip for vacation, the thought was now officially moved to the absolutely not column of things to do, right up there with jump out of an airplane or roll over Niagara Falls in a barrel. On the other hand, he was equally excited about seeing a real Texas ranch as his daughters were.

Following the directions on the GPS, along with Leah's notes on landmarks, the first thing to amaze him was how different things looked just a little north of the Houston city limits. It never would have occurred to him living the last several weeks in Houston that there were green rolling hills anywhere in the state. Apparently, today was destined to be a day of revelations. Once he turned off the main road, according to the GPS and Leah's landmarks, he found himself driving under a massive arch announcing the Paradise Ridge Ranch. That much was somehow expected in the great state of Texas, right along with yellow roses, long horn steers, and lone stars. What he had envisioned for the homestead was a reasonably large rustic home with a few barns and out houses. What came into view was much how he imagined Tara in *Gone With the Wind*. A massively large white home with tall columns suitable for the Parthenon. There had to be stables for the horses, but he couldn't see where from the long driveway.

"Oh, how pretty!" Hands on the glass, Michelle was pressed against the window.

Trish leaned over as far as her booster seat allowed. "Is this the White House?"

"No, sweetie." At this point that was the only thing Logan was sure of. Though the kid wasn't far off. The way Leah described her love for the family homestead, he expected something cozier, but as Trish had said, this place was indeed much more presidential than homestead.

The car had barely come to a stop when the front door opened wide and Leah came trotting down the steps. Opening the back car door, her smile was more radiant than ever. "Welcome to Paradise Ridge."

Buckles unsnapped, the girls scurried out of their seats, almost leap frogging over each other to run up to Leah and smother her in a waist-pinching hug.

"I think that means they approve." Logan still wasn't sure what he thought of all this. He'd always heard politics was a great way to get rich, but he only thought that applied to federal levels of government with lifetime pensions.

"Come inside for a minute. My grandparents want to meet you. Then my cousin Mitch has agreed to help us pick out the best horses for you."

She didn't need to say that twice. A child in each hand, the three females walked up the steps and into the home as if this was an everyday occurrence. The clichéd advice from years ago, one hand or one parent short, once again came to mind. Only this time, something told him that no matter how many kids she had, Leah would never come up short.

All it took was one foot in the door and one good look for him to be smacked with another surprise. The massive home indicative of wealth and opulence from the mere grandeur of the exterior was the polar opposite inside. Yes, the foyer was most likely bigger than his living room, but somehow it felt warm and receptive rather than cold and aloof. Quietly taking in the lovely furnishing and décor, all of which he was sure cost more than his annual salary, he wondered how had someone so good-natured and down to earth like Leah come from a world like this. A world so very different from his three bedroom, two bath upbringing.

"And you must be Miss Michelle and Miss Trish." A well dressed, but not overdressed, woman, who could be anywhere from sixty to eighty, grinned at his girls. At least he understood where Leah got her good naturedness from. And her warm smile.

"Hello." A man a few good years older than Leah walked into the foyer. "You must be the young ladies who have come to see our horses?"

Both girls bobbed their heads repeatedly.

"I'm Mitch." After shaking Logan's hand, he squatted down to not tower over them. "I'm going to take you to the stables. There are going to be a few rules though before we go over."

Again, the girls nodded.

While he explained the rules about not touching certain things, and where they should stand, and what horses could see, Leah came up beside him.

"Mitch is great with horses and kids."

His mind ran through the names she'd mentioned in passing and finally this one clicked. Senator Mitchell Baron. The man gave him pause. He seemed so genuine and warm and, well, nice. Maybe there was hope for the politicians in this country after all.

The rules speech over, Mitch stood erect and extended a hand to each girl. "Shall we go?"

Already several yards ahead of them, his daughters had to practically skip to keep up with Mitch's long stride. Or perhaps he was the one who had to extend his stride to keep up with their excited skips. The walk from the house to the stables wasn't long, but it wasn't short either. They'd left the house via a rear veranda and walked a reasonable distance over rolling green lawns when the stable came into sight.

"This is very impressive."

Leah shrugged. "To us, it's home."

"How long was your grandfather governor?"

"Sixteen years. I think the citizens of Texas would have voted him in for sixteen more if he'd been willing to run."

"I should go into politics."

"Excuse me?"

"Sorry. Was thinking out loud. I didn't realize how lucrative politics is in our country."

She shrugged. "That may be true, but politics isn't what bought this."

"Sorry, no offense meant."

"None taken."

"If it's none of my business, just say so, but what else did your grandfather do besides be governor?"

She sucked in a long breath and briefly squeezing her eyes shut, slowly blew it out. "Have you ever heard of Baron Industries?"

He almost said no, and then taking a moment to think, he remembered. "You mean the hotel consortium?"

Her head bobbed.

Another long moment of silence passed as he connected the dots of the conversation. "Those Barons are your family?"

Again, her head moved up and down. "Only the Barons didn't buy any of this. Paradise Ridge has been in my grandmother's family for generations."

"I see." He swallowed hard as they crossed into the barn. His neighbor wasn't a nice, helpful, and pretty lady, she was a full-blown heiress. What the heck was he doing here?

CHAPTER ELEVEN

It didn't take a genius to figure out that Leah's little revelation about her family had made Logan at least a tad uncomfortable. She supposed that was better than money hungry, but she already knew what a good man he was. If she had even a wisp of an inkling that he would want her for her money, she would never have brought up Baron Industries.

"Are those new boots on the girls?" She had to shift the conversation. The unease was thick enough to cut with the proverbial knife. "I love the colors."

To her relief, Logan smiled widely. "They insisted on shopping for boots. I had to talk them out of new jeans. After all, jeans are jeans."

She chuckled. "That might be a point of contention with a few of the wranglers, but for the most part, agreed."

"Thankfully, I convinced them about the jeans, but I felt that around horses, boots might be a better idea than their sneakers."

"It's more than just the horses stepping on you, it's what you step in that can be a challenge, from hay to you-know-what."

Chuckling, he nodded. "You learn something new every day raising girls. I thought a nice sensible pair of brown boots."

This time Leah laughed out loud. "Yeah, that wasn't going to happen. My favorite pair were pink with yellow flowers and big green leaves."

"Okay, now I don't feel so bad about what they picked."

Michelle's were a light gray with purple swirls stitched

on. Like a good seven-year-old, Trish had chosen a pink pair with fringe, but no obnoxious flowers.

Inside the barn, Mitch already had the girls at his side, explaining once again the dos and don'ts of handling horses. The ranch foreman had the mounting block set up. Leah hadn't seen that thing in so many years, she wondered if it was the same one she and her siblings and cousins had used to mount horses when they were too small to mount on their own.

"They're going to ride?" Logan's jaw almost hit the floor.

"Isn't that why they're here?"

Panic lit his eyes. "I thought it was to *see* the horses."

"What fun is that if you don't ride?"

"Daddy." Trish ran over, practically bouncing in place. "Mister Mitch says we can ride." Spinning about, she threw her arms around Leah's waist, squeezed her hard, and then still holding on, lifted her face to see Leah. "Thank you so much."

Before Leah could respond, the child had released her hold and turned to run back to her sister.

"I guess it's too late to put my foot down now." Panic in Logan's eyes had given way to something between fear and resignation.

"It will be fine. Honestly. We all started on horseback much younger than they are."

"How much younger?"

Tilting her head, she gazed up at him. "By three we all knew how to ride, and by five we were doing rodeos."

"Rodeos?" His voice actually squeaked.

"Relax, Dad." She patted his shoulder, gently running her hand down his arm, startled at the way her fingertips actually tingled at the connection.

"Which one of you wants to lead Trish?" Mitch stared over at the two of them.

"I will," Leah called out.

Logan glanced her way. "Lead?"

"We're going to start slow, walk them around the paddock, it's easy. It will be better if you cheer them both on from the sidelines. It would be harder to walk her and praise them both."

His head bobbed, even though he didn't look totally convinced.

"Remember how I taught you to hold the reins." Mitch instructed as the horses ambled out of the stables.

Noticing Trish was almost strangling the leather straps in her grip, Leah decided to reinforce the instructions. "If you pull too tightly, the horses will stop walking. We don't want that."

"Yes, Miss Leah." Trish looked totally confident, her body even swayed with the rhythm of the horse.

"Good job, you two," Leah encouraged.

A loud piercing whistle sounded and while the girls smiled and grinned, Leah looked to Logan just in time to see his fingers hanging from the corners of his mouth as another loud whistle reached her ears.

If the guy was still nervous, it didn't show anymore. All she saw was an amazingly supportive father. Logan may face multiple challenges as a single parent, but as far as Leah was concerned, he nailed fatherhood.

Pride oozed from every one of Logan's pores, seriously outweighing the fear he'd had over his precious little girls on such massive beasts. Booted foot—yeah, he'd bought a pair too—on the lower rail, he leaned over the fence surrounding the paddock, his heart swelling at the bright grins on Michelle and Trish's faces.

When Leah's gaze momentarily met his and her smile brightened, his heart did a two-step. He wasn't sure if it was his imagination, or just the man in him, but under the Texas sun, in blue jeans and a cowboy hat, Leah looked absolutely radiant. There wasn't a movie star or beauty queen who could outdo her beauty at this moment.

The girls time on the horses flew by. To his surprise, Mitch took them through the steps of caring for the horses after the ride. Considering the girls balked when he asked them to put their clothes in the hamper, or put their dishes in the sink, he was amazed at how easily and willingly they went through the paces with brushing and putting away the large animals.

"They're naturals." Leah sidled up beside him in the barn doorway while the girls, Mitch, and the foreman did their thing. "I don't know how much you know about riding, but those girls sit a horse well. Even Trish learned not only how to hold the reins, but how to use them. Did you notice when she wanted the horse to turn, how she tugged the reins to one side?"

He couldn't say that he had. As a matter of fact, the only horses he'd ever ridden were the quarter carousels outside the grocery store when he was a toddler. "Can't say that I did, but they certainly looked like they were having fun."

"They were." She leaned up against him a minute, her hand landing on his forearm. "You've got great kids, you know."

"I do." As much as he'd love to take credit for it, he felt that Deb deserved the recognition. Not only did she spend quality time with them while he worked all day, but after she was gone, the girls seemed to worry more about taking care of him than themselves. "Very good kids."

"If y'all want to stick around for dinner, there's plenty of room at the table."

His knee-jerk reaction was to offer a polite no thank you, but the truth was he really wanted to spend more time with her, even if it meant being surrounded by a former governor and a roomful of her family. He also knew the girls would just love it. "Thank you, that would be nice."

His first impression of a warm home was reinforced the second they entered the large family room scattered with comfortable furniture or happily chattering family. There was nothing stuffy or pretentious about the décor or the family. Two gentlemen, one of which he seemed to remember was introduced as Leah's brother, played checkers at a small table by the window. The two hooted and hollered as if they were ten years old and playing for the world title. The interaction made him smile.

"Daddy, look." Michelle pointed to where the Governor and his wife sat, each with a tail-wagging dog at their side.

"Go on, honey." Mrs. Baron waved at the dog, who looked to be waiting for the command to bolt across and greet his girls.

With a wave of his hand and a nod, the Governor gave his dog permission to do the same.

Two eager, tail wagging dogs brushed up against the girls, licked them, and before he knew it, the four were in a huddle of laughter bouncing and wiggling all over the floor.

"What those two dogs needed," the Governor bobbed his chin, "was someone to play with. You and your girls are welcome any time, young man."

Young man. That made him smile even more. Not that Logan was an old goat or anything, but he hadn't been referred to as a young man since his first promotion a few eons ago. "Thank you, sir."

Halfway through dinner, despite the lively chatter at the large table brimming with Barons, droopy eyes began to set in. While Logan was in a politely heated discussion with Kyle over a differing opinion on one of his racing competitors, Leah was the first to notice the girls losing steam. What made him almost laugh was how Leah kicked him under the table, and then with a lift of her chin, directed his attention to his daughters.

"I think it's past someone's bedtime." Lila Baron smiled at the girls.

The Governor nodded. "Yes. We tend to forget that little ones need earlier lights out." Turning his attention to Mitch, the older man's smile spread across his face. "But soon, we'll be in the habit again."

Despite his daughters' objections, Logan decided that staying for dessert was not a good idea tonight.

Lila Baron brushed her hand gently along the side of Trish's face before cupping her chin and lifting the younger sister's face to meet hers. "I'm sure we can talk your father into letting you come back really soon."

Trish gave a very reluctant nod that totally belied her pouty lips.

"I'll tell you what." Lila pressed on. "What's your favorite dessert?"

Trish shouted, "Belgian waffles!" at the same time Michelle called out "Boston Cream Pie!"

Momentarily confused, Lila lifted her gaze to Logan. "Aren't you from California?"

Logan nodded. "The owner of the best bakery near our home is from Massachusetts."

"Ah." Lila returned her attention to the girls. "I bet we can get Hazel to make your favorite desserts the next time you come. Does that sound like fun?"

Instantly, smiles appeared on the two sisters' faces and their head moved up and down with such force, it wouldn't have surprised anyone if they'd merely snapped off.

"I'll follow you home." Leah grabbed her purse and hugged her grandmother. "See you next week."

Now Logan wished they'd come together instead of separate cars. The chance to spend a little more time with her on the drive would have been great. As it was, they'd park, say goodnight, and then he'd tuck the girls in. If only he could come up with a good reason to invite her to come in for coffee or a glass of wine. Anything that would give him even a few more minutes with her. A few more minutes? Wasn't that almost laughable? What the heck was going on with him?

CHAPTER TWELVE

Following Logan's taillights, Leah couldn't stop smiling. The only thing she wished is that she'd not spent the night at the ranch but had instead ridden with Logan this afternoon. Then she could be spending this time chatting with him rather than wishing she were with him in the car.

Lots of thoughts ran through her mind right now. Starting with what a wonderful time she'd had walking and talking with Logan and teaching the girls how to ride. As silly as it sounded, she was actually a pinch jealous not to have been able to go with the girls shopping for their first pair of cowboy boots. She still remembered how much fun she had that day with her grandmother when she bought those obnoxious pink boots with the three big flowers.

The entire ride home, her smile remained fixed as she reflected on what an all-around nice guy Logan was. Of all the men she dated after graduating college—because it was totally unfair to compare a grown man like Logan with the immature kids from high school or college kids finding their place in the world—no one had held her interest the way Logan does. And not a single one made her heart smile at the sight of him.

Logan turned into the building parking lot, and she pulled into the space beside him. Back door on the driver side open, he stood, head tilted slightly, staring into the car.

"Something wrong?" She hopped out of the car and hurried to his side, immediately spotting his dilemma. Both of his daughters were soundly asleep. "You run upstairs and unlock the door, and I'll wait here. When you get back you can carry Michelle, I'll carry Trish."

"Good idea letting me open the door. It's been a while but when they were younger there was nothing worse than trying to juggle a kid and keys. But I can take them both, you don't have to carry them too."

"It's late and they are obviously very tired, I don't mind helping at all."

For just a moment he hesitated, and she thought he was going to argue. But then he nodded, turned on his heel, and hurried up the stairs. By the time he'd come down, she had already unsnapped Trish's safety belt from the booster seat, and frankly, was a tad surprised that the little girl didn't flinch.

"Are you sure you don't want to wait for me to come back and get her?" Logan already had Michelle unstrapped.

Hefting Trish out of the car and onto her shoulder, she kicked the door shut with her foot and smiled at him. "I got this."

Inside the apartment, they headed to the bedroom. Laying the girls down, they first slipped off one shoe then the other. Afterwards, Leah awkwardly tugged down Trish's blue jeans, then frowning, looked up at Logan and whispered, "I can't believe she's still sleeping. Should we put them in their jammies, or is taking off her shoes and jeans enough?"

"I vote for this is fine. If we try to undress them the rest of the way to put their pajamas on, we could wake them up."

She nodded, kissed each girl on the cheek, then already knowing the routine from the other night, flipped on the switch to the white noise machine and left the room with Logan only a few steps behind her.

"Thanks for the help. I could have done it alone, but it was most definitely easier with an extra set of arms."

"My pleasure."

Almost at the front of the apartment, Logan smiled at her. "And thanks for such a great day. The girls had a blast. I did too."

"You and the girls have an open invitation to the ranch anytime you want. If their interest in horses doesn't turn out to be a fluke, my cousin Eve was an expert barrel racer, and I know she would just love to teach the girls."

Eyes open wide, he blinked at her. "Barrel racing?"

Leah lifted her hand to muffle her own laughter. "Sorry, too much too fast?"

His head bobbed. "Maybe. Yeah." Stretching his shoulders, and tilting his head left and right, he blew out a sigh. "I don't know about you, but I could use a good hot cup of coffee. Can I interest you in joining me?"

"Sounds lovely." She made herself at home on the loveseat while he moved about in the kitchen and then appeared two steaming mugs in hand, gave her one, and sat down beside her. "Thank you."

He merely nodded and she took in a deep breath. She'd expected him to sit in another seat. Having him close enough to touch made her heart beat just a little bit faster.

"You know." He briefly blew on the steaming liquid. "When I found out we had to leave California, I thought everything here was going to be so difficult. Our support system there was slim. Neither Deb nor I have a lot of family, but slim was better than nothing." A smile teased up one side of his mouth. "Who knew how wrong I was."

"Thank you, I think."

"Most definitely. You, and your family too, have been a huge blessing. The girls even called your sister the other day just to chat."

"They did?" Why did that thought unsettle her so? Claire was kind and friendly. So what if the girls liked her too? It wasn't a big deal, and yet, it felt like a big deal. Once again, that edge of jealousy raised its ugly head. She needed to get a grip.

Staring into his mug, he didn't look up. "Deb and I were high school sweethearts. The first minute I saw her standing at her locker our freshman year, my tongue stuck to the roof of my mouth."

Leah smiled. "That's sweet."

"Made it hard as hell to say hello. But eventually, I built up the nerve to talk to her. It took a while. That entire first year of high school, we became really good friends."

"The best relationships start with friendship. That's what Grams always says."

"I would have to agree with her." Cradling the mug, his eyes lifted to meet hers. "It never occurred to me that I would be able to find another connection like what I had with Deb."

"I understand."

"Do you?" His hand lifted, his fingers brushing a lock of hair behind her ear.

Her breath caught and she reminded herself to breathe.

"I know I'm a little old to be asking this, but it's all I know. May I kiss you?"

Now her tongue was stuck to the roof of her mouth, all she could do was nod.

Setting the mug down on the end table beside him, he turned toward her, his finger gently gliding down the side of her jaw, sending tingles all the way to her toes. Deep blue eyes leveled with hers. Easing closer, anticipation raced through her, his lips were so close she could feel the warmth radiating between them. Her heart beat like a banging drum. She was about to kiss this man who had been in her every waking thought for weeks. Her lids fell closed, her lips parted, and a blood-curdling scream pierced the air.

Not even when Logan's mother walked in and caught him and Deb making out when he was fifteen had he jumped off the sofa so fast.

Sprinting over the arm, Leah followed him down the hall and into the girls' room.

To his surprise, Michelle was still sound asleep. Only a kid could sleep through a scream like that. Trish, on the other hand, sat upright, and with her eyes closed, was sobbing heavily.

"Shh." Leah had his daughter fully embraced in her arms, gently patting her back, and even rocking in place. "Does anything hurt?"

His eyes popped open. It would never have occurred to him to find out if his daughter was in pain. Did little kids have ruptured appendixes? Or ear aches. As a toddler, Michelle suffered through lots of ear aches.

Now, sobbing into Leah's shoulder, Trish shook her head.

"Was it a bad dream?"

Trish nodded, still burying her face in Leah's shoulder.

"It's all right. The dream is over."

"Daddy…" she gulped air, "was in a car accident and died."

"Oh, baby. Your daddy is right here." Lifting her hand away from the little girl for a moment, she waved him over.

Logan sat on the edge of the bed beside Leah. "I'm perfectly safe, sweetie. I'm right here."

Through hiccupped breaths, Trish looked directly into Leah's eyes. "I don't want Daddy to go to heaven."

"No, baby." Leah shook her head and swept the hair out of Trish's eyes. "Daddy's not going to heaven yet. Not until you and Michelle are grown up with grandbabies of your own."

That seemed to give the little girl pause. Still sucking in tattered breaths, her gaze narrowed. "Will you stay with us if Daddy goes to heaven?"

He couldn't see the look on Leah's face, but the request had certainly grabbed him by the heart strings.

"Of course I will, but it doesn't matter because your daddy isn't going anywhere anytime soon."

"Promise?" Trish finally seemed to be taking regular breaths.

Leah hesitated and Logan figured she didn't like making a promise she had no way of knowing if she could keep. After all, Deb would have made the same promise before they lost her, never knowing what was waiting around the corner. "I promise."

Her breaths slowing even more, Trish pulled away and looked at her father. "I love you, Daddy."

"I love you too, Princess."

Without another word, Trish laid back on the pillow and

closed her eyes. Both he and Leah stayed in their spots on the bed until the heavy rhythm of deep breathing told them that Trish had fallen back asleep.

Slowly, they tiptoed out of the room, closed the door, and continued their soft steps down the hall.

"I knew that losing their mom was probably harder on the girls than even on me." Logan sat in the love seat where they'd been seated before. "I thought they were too young for grief counseling."

"I don't know." Leah shook her head. "Does she have nightmares a lot?"

He shook his head. "I wonder what prompted this one?"

"Also out of my wheelhouse. I know lawyers, judges, briefs, witnesses, and jurors, but little girls are not my strength."

"Could have fooled me. You did better than I would have."

"I doubt that. I just did what instinct told me."

"That's pretty much how parenting works, then we pray we're not screwing up our kids for the rest of their lives."

"I bet."

He rubbed the bare finger where his wedding ring had sat for so long. "It was a quick run to the grocery store. Took me a while to even notice how long Deb had been gone before I picked up the phone to call her. Thought maybe she'd had a flat or something." He raised his gaze from his finger to Leah. "A policeman answered."

Blowing out a sigh, she closed her eyes tightly before opening them again. "I'm sorry."

"I was in shock for days, then I realized it was weeks, and eventually months. Not really sure when I fully snapped out of it."

"These things take time."

He inhaled and then exhaled. "There were times I wondered if I'd ever get over losing her."

"I can imagine."

"I think leaving California and all things familiar, all the memories, was my first test. Moving here, setting up the apartment, settling in with the girls, I realized for the first time, though I'll always miss Deb, I no longer *missed* her. Does that make sense?"

"Maybe."

"At every turn that first year, I thought of Deb, wished she were here, wondered what she would do. By the time we moved here, that didn't happen any more. Now I'm wondering just when did I stop thinking about her all the time."

Leah nodded.

He very much wanted to kiss her right now, but somehow, it simply didn't feel right anymore. But he sure hoped it would feel right soon. Very soon.

CHAPTER THIRTEEN

Almost a week had passed since the day of riding, the bad dream, and the almost kiss. Leah had replayed those few seconds before the scream over and over in her mind. At one point, she was working on a brief and somehow had their defendant kissing the plaintiff. How she changed hitting to kissing was purely a matter of her having kissing on the brain. Kissing Logan Miller.

A light rap sounded against her door.

"Come in."

"Hey." Her assistant entered carrying a folder. "Have you considered it might be a good day for some R&R?"

"What?" She frowned. "No. I have so much work I may not catch up before the next millennium."

"Mm." Jeffrey dropped a file on her desk. "Fortunately, I looked that over before submitting it to Mr. Lansing."

Leah closed her eyes. What had she done?

"You know how you recommended group mediation?"

She nodded.

Jeffrey shook his head. "Group Meditation."

"A typo. Blast." Stupid proofing software was virtually useless.

Again Jeffrey shook his head. "Seven times."

Oh, hell. Maybe she did need a day off. "Thanks. I think I will take the afternoon off. Leave that on my desk and I'll fix it." She grabbed her purse out of the desk and pushed to her feet. "As a matter of fact, I won't be back till Monday."

"Good idea." Jeffrey smiled. "The world will not end. I promise."

I promise. Her mind turned to Trish. Maybe she could convince Logan to let her take the girls out shopping, or to the ranch, or…whatever.

Briefcase in hand, she made her way out of the building and into her car, tossed the briefcase onto the front seat, slid inside and throwing her head back, blew out a deep breath. "So, woman, now what?" Straightening in her seat, she reached for her phone, about to dial Logan, when the thing vibrated in her hand. Speak of the devil. "Hello."

"Hey," Logan's voice rolled over her like a comfortable old blanket. "Sorry to bother you at work."

"No bother. I'm actually on my way home."

"Really? You feeling all right?" The deep concern in his voice made her smile.

"Feeling fine." Technically. It was just her brains and her hormones that were scrambled. "Just time for a day off. What can I do for you?"

"Day off, huh?"

"Yes. Is something wrong?"

"No. I was calling to see about when I could bring the girls for the horses again. That is all they talked about every minute for days."

"This Saturday or Sunday would be fine."

"Thank you. That would be great, but I was just thinking…"

"Yes?"

"I was just thinking that it's too pretty a day to be cooped up inside. Any chance I can convince you to play hooky with me and spend the afternoon at the beach? I hear Galveston is an interesting little town."

"Yes, it is, but full disclosure, the Galveston Coast won't compare with the California beaches."

"I've been told. Interested?"

Was she? Looking up at the clear blue sky and then over to her briefcase, she smiled. "Absolutely."

The last thing Logan thought when he woke up this morning was that he'd be spending the day with Leah. At the beach, no less.

Her head back, her eyes closed, she looked like an angel. Maybe that was it. Maybe she was his guardian angel and he was just fooling himself into believing she was a mere mortal.

One eye opened and she glanced over at him. "Did I fall asleep?"

"Yep."

"Sorry." She scooted upright. "Oh, we're here. Do you want to hit the strand or the beach first?"

Took him a minute. "I think the beach would be a nice treat."

"Okay, stay on the freeway and then we'll turn at the seawall."

From there, he followed her instructions, pulled down a sandy dirt road and parked feet away from the shore. The moment she stepped out of the car, he realized how inappropriate his choice had been. Since they hadn't gone home to change, she wore a flared skirt below the knees, a pristine pressed shirt and a loose jacket with the sleeves rolled up to three quarters and heels. At least he had been dressed down today in jeans and dock shoes. "We should have probably stopped home to change."

She shook her head. "Nah." Opening the back door of the car, she took off her jacket and tossed it in the back seat. "Let's go."

"But your shoes?" He waved an arm at her feet.

"No problem." She walked down the unleveled road with the poise of a model on a high fashion runway. The moment they reached the actual shore, she grabbed his arm with one hand and leaned over, pulling off her shoes, then straightened, holding the shoes in one hand. "Ready."

The hand on his arm slid away and immediately he missed the feel of her on him. Taking in a deep breath, he looked off into the distance and then taking a chance, reached over and took hold of her hand, then facing her, held up their clasped hands. "Is this okay?"

A slight smile crossed her lips. "More than all right."

They'd walked a while in silence. He suspected she was

as much in need of a little vitamin sea as he had been.

"Penny for your thoughts?" she asked softly.

Slowing his casual pace a bit more, he shrugged. "You really want to know?"

"I wouldn't have asked if I didn't."

"Okay. How come there isn't a man in your life?"

"Ah." She bobbed her chin. "Truth?"

"And nothing but."

She chuckled as he'd hoped. "Being a Baron can intimidate a lot of men, throw in a legal career, a damn good litigator no less, and well…"

Having spent an afternoon with her family on a very impressive ranch, he could see where that would be the case.

"And then, the real challenge is those who are a little too in love with the Baron name."

Aha. He should have thought of that. "And their money."

"That about nails it." She chuckled a little more loudly. "It was actually a relief that when I gave you my name, you had no idea who I was related to. It was kind of nice to know someone got along with me for the real me. I don't think I've had that since I was a kid in school."

"Not to sound like an old cliché, but for those who don't appreciate the real you, it's their loss."

"Thank you."

He came to a stop and spun her around to face him. Probably a little harder than he should have because she dropped her shoes. High fashion wasn't his strength, but even he knew those red soles were not cheap. And yet, here she was, strolling down the beach like any ordinary person. In the middle of the week, in the off season, there wasn't another person on the beach, just a few squawking seagulls. "About the other night."

"Yes?"

This time he didn't bother with a request, he simply dipped his head to meet her lips. Gently, and slowly, more out of fear than caution, his mouth pressed against hers. He let go of her hand and wrapping his arms around her waist, tugged her in closer. Her entire body melted against him as the kiss took on a life of its own.

Squawking overhead grew louder and he didn't care. At this moment, all he wanted was to stand here with the sand under their feet, the sun at their backs and the ocean breeze blanketing them. Too bad the birds had other ideas. One flew so close he could feel the rush of wind beside his shoulder. Another moment and one came near enough to slap his head with its wings.

Pulling back to wave off the obnoxious birds, another one came whizzing by reminding him of a kamikaze pilot. "What the heck?" Wrapping her against him, he tucked her to one side to protect her. "What is the matter with these birds?"

To his surprise, she laughed into his shoulder. "Be thankful you're not eating. They can be vicious creatures. I've had them pick food off my plate and peck at my head for not sharing."

"You're kidding?"

She laughed even harder. "I wish I were."

Resigned that this was not the place for another kissing session, he took her hand and began walking back up the beach.

It had been a very long time since he was so comfortable in silence. As if reading his thoughts, her cell phone buzzed, breaking the comfortable silence.

Leah reached into her pocket, scanned the screen, frowned and texted back, before looking up at him. "How do you feel about tuxedos?"

"Like a penguin."

That made her chuckle. "Grams just reminded me that there's a benefit tomorrow night for one of her favorite charities. These galas get really boring really fast sometimes."

"I bet."

"Any chance I can talk you into joining me? It's black-tie so you'll have to rent a tux."

"Don't have to rent. Already own a tux."

"You do?" Her eyes rounded like silver dollars.

"Don't look so surprised. There was a point in time where we went to so many weddings and business banquets that I broke down and bought my own tux."

"So, is that a yes?"

Chuckling, he nodded.

"Yay!" She threw her arms around him and kissed him quickly and hard on the lips. "Thank you."

Even if she didn't know it yet, he knew that whatever she wanted, he would give her. After Deb, it never occurred to him he could ever feel that way about anyone else. And yet, here was willing to dress up like a penguin and if she'd asked, fly to the moon for the party. All he could do now is pray that revelation wouldn't scare her as much as it scared him.

CHAPTER FOURTEEN

"I don't know about this." Logan repeated, not for the first time.

"Are you kidding? My grandparents are over the moon at the thought of having little ones in the house, even if they're not home." At such short notice, Logan was unable to find a trusted babysitter for the gala, and, of course, Claire couldn't fill in because she, along with half the Baron family, was attending the gala. That left one solution, bringing the girls to the ranch and leaving Hazel in charge. "Hazel has teaching the girls how to make their favorite desserts all planned out. You saw how happy she was to have the girls in her kitchen. I'm not sure who's more excited about this little sleepover, my grandparents or Hazel."

"I know that in my head, but I can't help but feel that just dropping them off for the night is an imposition."

"Well, you only have one choice." Tearing her gaze away from the road, she briefly cast a sideways glance at him, grinning as brightly as she could. "Get over it."

As she had hoped, Logan spit out a laugh. "I suppose you are right."

"Of course I'm right. If there's one thing I know, it's my family." And she was starting to truly understand Logan Miller. Of the handful of men she had dated in the last few years, not a single one would she have been able to tell them to just *get over it.* She loved how in these few short weeks, she and Logan had become such good friends. And the kissing was a pretty cool perk too. Between the beach, supper on the Strand, tucking the girls into bed, and saying goodnight to each other, they had managed to get in some pretty sweet kissing. If she'd learned anything the last few weeks, it was that life was too short to spend so much of it sitting behind a desk. She couldn't remember ever being this happy with a man. The intelligent adult in her knew Logan had flaws—everyone had flaws, not even her grandparents were an exception to that—but so far, Logan was proving to be a considerate, thoughtful man, a good father, a good neighbor, and a good friend. She pretty much loved everything about him.

Loved? Love. Her grip on the steering wheel tightened. Exactly how much did she love Logan? Was it even possible to fall in love with someone in weeks? Didn't most people need months and months, or even years to fall fully and wholly in love with another person? Her mind darted back and forth from one cousin to another. The ones who had all met, fallen in love with, and married in less than a year. A few in only months. Good grief.

"You still with us?" Logan's voice broke through her thoughts.

"Excuse me?" She blinked, clearing her thoughts.

His shoulders barely moving from withholding a chuckle, Logan smiled at her. "You did not hear a word I said, did you?"

"I'm sorry. I guess I was just thinking ahead."

His hand reached across the bucket seats and captured hers. "It's going to be a great night. Ever since the plans were set earlier today, the girls have done nothing but talk about learning to cook with Hazel. I don't think I've ever seen anybody more excited to be led into the kitchen to start baking. And Hazel looked pretty darn excited herself. It looks like you were right. I shouldn't have worried. Anyone would think both my girls had won the lottery."

"I'm sure that's how they feel."

"I suppose I should probably start working on helping them learn their way around a kitchen more. I didn't realize they had an interest. Not that my skills are that great, but we're not starving."

"Your skills are wonderful." She grinned at him from ear to ear and would swear she saw a flash of pink tinge the tips of his ears. One more positive quality to add to the growing list of the good things about Logan Miller.

This was not the first time that Logan had to attend a fancy or elegant party, but he had to admit, this was by far one of the most elaborate and dazzling events he'd ever been to. There was little doubt not a single man here had rented his tuxedo, and judging by the blinding bling on some of the women, there was plenty of money to burn.

"Isn't it just lovely?" Lila Baron scanned the room. "The children's hospital is going to get that new cardiac unit. I can feel it in my bones."

"A worthy cause." He hoped she was right. Who didn't have a soft spot for sick children.

"One of your new grandsons?" A tall woman with enough diamonds dripping around her neck to sink the Titanic came up to Mrs. Baron.

"No, Ida. This is a friend of Leah's."

"Friend?" The woman raised her brows. "Do you dance?"

"I've been told that's a matter of opinion." No point in mentioning that according to his late wife he could cut the rug better than anyone they knew.

"Only one way to find out." The older woman actually batted her lashes at him.

"I'd be delighted." He extended his elbow to the woman and leaned back toward Mrs. Baron. "If you'll excuse me, and also please tell Leah where I've gone?"

"Of course." Lila nodded, then just as he thought she was about to kiss his cheek, she whispered, "Deep pockets, see if you can loosen her purse strings."

He almost laughed out loud. Not sure what he could do, but he was willing to give it a shot.

As he twirled the woman he now knew was Ida Thornwood around the floor, he did his best to sing the praises of the children's hospital and how wonderful all these people cared about sick children.

"Are you giving to the hospital?"

"Absolutely." And he would. "No amount is too much for a worthy cause."

The woman smiled but seemed to be thinking. He hoped favorably.

As the second song began, he realized Mrs. Thornwood had no intention of sitting down and was resigned to another spin around the floor when he felt a soft tap on his shoulder.

"Excuse me, but I believe I have the next dance." Leah stood smiling at the other woman.

"Oh, of course, dear." Mrs. Thornwood stepped back. "And if my opinion counts, you're a wonderful dancer."

Logan smiled. "Thank you."

As the other woman walked away, he scooped Leah into the fold of his arms and happily danced across the floor.

"Okay, I'm in with Ida. You are a really good dancer."

"My mother swore taking dance lessons would make me popular with the ladies."

"Was she right?"

"No idea, but Deb never complained."

Leah grinned at him. "Smart woman."

He loved that he could talk to her about Deb, mention her in passing, and it never seemed to upset Leah. At times, she even delicately asked questions. Seemed to want to know more about Deb, to help keep her memory alive with the girls. One more detail to add to the list of things that made Leah Baron so special.

"Sorry, dear." Lila Baron pulled the two aside of the dance floor. "I have no idea what you said to that stingy woman, but Ida just pledged a hundred thousand dollars. All I can say is, would you please dance with the other rich tightwads?"

Chuckling, he shrugged. "Sure. If it helps."

"Oh, good." Rubbing her hands together, Lila Baron practically floated off the dance floor.

"You do realize she's not kidding?" Leah actually

looked worried.

"If she is, it's for a good cause." He paused, all humor gone. "Unless you'd rather I didn't?"

"If you're okay with it, I'm okay with it." She lifted onto her tippy toes and gently kissed his lips quickly. "You're a nice man, Logan Miller."

"You're a special lady, Leah Baron." With that, he twirled her again and waltzed deeper onto the floor until someone else pulled him away.

Three ladies and two glasses of champagne later, he found himself at the bar with some of Leah's family while Leah cut the rug with her grandfather.

"You doing okay?" Her brother Cooper took a sip of his drink.

"Shouldn't I be?"

"All this polite party talk can wear a person out. Besides, I hear that Grams has lassoed you into sweet-talking the rich widows."

"There was no lassoing involved. It's my pleasure to help."

Cooper nodded. "Good to hear."

"We appreciate that you're being such a good sport about this." Chase, one of Leah's cousins, patted him on the shoulder. "Not that we all don't do what we can for worthy causes, but you're a better dancer than any of us," the man joked.

"And better looking too." Leah came up to him and put her hand on his forearm. "Are they treating you right?"

"Always." Cooper raised his glass and Chase merely smiled.

"I'll have you know, Grams said they've already passed the hospital's goal for the night and there's still hours to go."

"I guess you'd better get back to dancing," Chase laughed.

"Those women will have to get in line." Leah grabbed his hand. "My turn."

On the dance floor, he held her much closer than he had the merry widows. "Are you having a good time?"

"Actually," her eyes twinkled, "I am."

"I feel bad leaving you to your own devices, when the whole reason I was invited was to keep you company."

She shook her head. "No. What you're doing is important, and the fact that you're happy helping makes me happy."

"It's actually quite fascinating."

"What is?"

"Talking with these women. They may have a great deal of money to give away, but they're just like anyone else. I admit Ida was a tad intimidating, but once I realized all I had to do was talk to them the way I would my Aunt Lisa, or my mom, things went just fine." They did a spin to avoid being too close to the other dancers. "It's rather a relief to know that the ultra-rich aren't that different from the ultra ordinary."

"Or the ultra ordinary aren't that different from the ultra-rich," she said.

Delighted when the orchestra shifted to a slow ballad, Logan pulled Leah even closer to him. Everything about her fit so perfectly against him, he wanted desperately to steal a real kiss. "What time does this shindig end?"

"Officially at midnight, but we can gracefully leave without repercussions after ten."

"Would you mind if we don't stay till the end?"

Her smile widened. "You're reading my mind. I was thinking maybe you might not be too tired to come over to my place for a night cap, or a hot chocolate?"

"Hot chocolate and turning on the gas logs sounds heavenly. As long as I can take off my tie."

"You can change into anything you want, just don't change who you are."

"Back at you, Leah. Stay just the way you are."

There was no point in adding, *here in my arms, preferably forever.* Because whether he'd known it when he put on this monkey suit or not, he understood now that he didn't just like Leah as a friend or a date, he loved her with or without money, and with or without a large involved family. Now, he needed to help her fall for him too. All he had to figure out was how.

CHAPTER FIFTEEN

Sun crept across the room, slowly dragging Leah from her dreams of dancing on a cloud with Logan. Last night had been the most fun she'd had at a charity event since she was deemed old enough to dress up and attend posh galas with the family. At first, she'd been awed by the beautiful gowns and exciting people. Eventually, these events fell into the category of same old, same old. Until last night.

Stretching her arms and looking at her bedside clock with one eye, she frowned and wondered if she could possibly sneak in another thirty minutes of sleep. Turning onto her side and pounding her pillow, she'd snuggled under the covers when the front doorbell rang, killing any plans for more sleep. Throwing back the blankets and slipping into her robe, she hurried to the door and swinging it open, smiled like a loon at the sight of Logan holding up two paper bags.

"I didn't know if you preferred an egg and sausage croissant, a breakfast burrito, or donuts."

"Can I have it all?" She waved him into the apartment, thoroughly delighted when he paused to lean in and kiss her briefly on the lips.

"Absolutely." Setting the bags on the kitchen island, he turned to face her. "I called the ranch, spoke to Hazel, she said that the girls were up bright and early helping her make breakfast but neither of your grandparents had come downstairs yet. Apparently, we have created monsters."

"Monsters?" Holding the donut in her hand, she took a bite.

"I've been informed the girls want to take cooking classes."

"Do they have cooking classes for kids that young?" She took another bite. She knew she should start the day with a little protein, like the burrito, but who could resist warm glazed donut?

He shrugged. "I have no earthly idea, but it looks like I'm going to find out."

As Leah reached for the burrito and took a bite, in the back of her mind she could hear her grandmother's voice echoing: you're not a raccoon, use a knife and fork. She'd barely swallowed the hand-held morsel when the phone rang and her grandmother's name appeared on the caller ID. Not for the first time, Leah actually considered that maybe her grandmother was psychic. "Hello."

"Good morning, dear." The sound of giggles in the background came through the line. "The girls just made the most delicious pancakes. Mitch and Gwyneth are going to give them another lesson in the paddock, so there's no hurry to pick them up. Unless you're hungry. In which case, come on over, and, of course, Logan, too."

"Thanks, Grams. I'm already eating, but I'll let Logan know."

"Of course, dear, and thank you." Her words were delivered with the same aplomb her grandmother always managed, but Leah could hear the woman smiling clear through the phone.

"What are you going to let me know? Are the girls too much?" His brows curled together. "Are they okay?"

"Relax, Dad. They're perfectly fine. Sounds like maybe too fine. They're cooking, and getting ready to go horse back riding again, and I suspect if we don't go pick them up soon, they may never want to come home."

"Got it." He nodded, then the smile returned. "They really do like your family."

"So do I." She took another bite and reached for the coffee.

He laughed a little louder. "Then it's unanimous, because so do I."

"Really?" She could feel her cheeks tugging at the corners of her mouth. Having someone truly like her and her family for who they were, not for their money or connections, was almost euphoric.

"Why is that so hard to believe?" His brows dipped into a Vee again and he sighed. "Sorry. I forgot about the money thing."

Almost spewing coffee across the room, she swallowed hard and laughed heartily. "And *that's* why I love you. You may be the only person on the planet who forgets about the Baron money."

A stone-like expression took over his face. Not sure what had him suddenly turn so serious, she was even more surprised when he not only came close, but cupping her face in his hands, leaned in and kissed her so sweet and intense that her toes actually curled in her slippers.

When he inched away, her eyes slowly opened, staring into the warmest eyes and sweetest smile. "What was that for?"

"I love you too."

Shock that she'd accidentally declared her feelings out loud shot through her system, rendering her momentarily silent. Not till her mind registered what he'd actually responded—he loved her too—did the shock give way to sheer joy.

His thumb ran down her cheek and across her tingling lips. "I'd like to discuss this new revelation more, but I think we should get the girls first."

"Yes," she nodded, "the girls. You're probably right." She forced herself to take a step in retreat. "I'll get dressed. We'll go get them."

She had barely climbed out of the shower when her phone rang again. Her grandmother once more. "Have you left the house yet?"

There had barely been time to drink her coffee or kiss Logan, never mind shower, dress, and leave. "Not yet."

"Oh, good. Claire is here and she says she'll bring the girls. They've asked her to take them shopping for a few things on the way home rather than ride the horses, so expect them soon but not too soon."

"Got it. I'll tell Logan."

"You do that." Again, her grandmother's voice was very calm, but Leah could still hear the smile.

Claire had called to give Logan a heads up that they were pulling into the parking lot of the apartment complex and could use some help. Turning to Leah, he cocked his head to one side. "Did anyone tell you what Claire took the girls shopping for?"

"Nope." She shook her head.

He stared down at this phone. "They're in the parking lot and Claire needs help. I'm going to head on downstairs." He kissed Leah on the tip of her nose. "I'll call you a little later?"

Her head bobbed up and down and her sweet smile had him wanting to pull her into his arms and kiss her senseless, but fatherhood called.

At the bottom of the stairs, he saw Claire pull into the nearest empty space. Her choice of vehicle surprised him. He expected a sleek foreign car, maybe even a sports car, not a massive quad cab pickup.

"Daddy!" The girls ran up to him.

"We had so much fun!" Michelle practically squealed.

"Can we go back soon?" Trish asked. "Hazel is as nice as Grams."

"Grams?" he looked to Claire.

"Apparently," Leah's sister shrugged, smiled, and handed him two bags from a local grocer, "they've been adopted into the family."

What felt like twenty or thirty bags of groceries later, Claire gave the girls a quick kiss on the cheek and said her goodbyes, then turned to him from her car. "Enjoy!"

He nodded before he realized he had no idea what she was talking about. All anyone would say when he asked what this was all about, was that it was a surprise. He wasn't even allowed to help put away whatever they'd bought. A time or two he tried to sneak into the kitchen and was shooed back into the living room. At one point the girls got tired of dealing with him.

"Dad, why don't you go visit Leah?" The look of exasperation on Michelle's face almost had him laughing.

"What are you two up to?"

"We told you." Both of Trish's fists landed at her waist. "It's a surprise."

Next thing he knew, the two were literally shoving him out the door and before he could object, they'd closed it behind him and turned the lock. With no other choice, he knocked on Leah's door.

"Back so soon?"

"I've been evicted."

"What?" Her jaw dropped and her eyes widened.

He shot both his hands up, palms out, shaking his head. "Not by the landlord, by my daughters."

Covering her mouth, she tried to camouflage her laughter. "I see."

Looking around, he hovered by the front door. "I can't decide if I should sit down and let them do their thing, or go back and remind them who is the head of the family."

Shaking her head and trying not to laugh, she patted his arm. "Why don't you have a seat. I'll make a pot of coffee and then you can go check on the progress."

"They are only seven and nine."

Her head bobbed. "It's no different than when they wake up at six in the morning and turn on the television while you're in the other room sound asleep until eight. You're only across the hall. They'll be fine for a short while."

"I suppose." He sighed heavily. "This single parenting thing is rough on the nerves."

"And you're doing a great job."

"Thanks."

The coffee brewed, she'd barely handed him the warm mug when she heard rustling by her door. "I wonder if it's time for you to go home?" Setting her own mug on the end table, she walked over to the door and glanced out the peephole. Nothing.

Logan was on his feet. "Are they there?"

"No." She took a step back and spotted a piece of paper on the floor. An index card. "What's this?"

Stepping away from the sofa, Logan appeared beside her, reading the crayon-written card out loud.

Your presents has been requested for brunch at the Miller restaurant. Please come.

"Except for misspelling presence, not bad." Logan nodded a second before his eyes flew open into perfectly round orbs. "They can't be cooking!"

His hand reached for the doorknob and she grabbed it. "Hang on. Deep breath. If they are well enough to slip an invitation under my door, they are not bleeding, burned, or anything else unpleasant."

"I suppose. But the invitation does say please come. Can we go now?"

Chuckling, she patted his arm. "Yes. We can go now."

The man practically pulled her front door off the hinges in his hurry to get home and check on his precious girls. She couldn't blame him. Depending on what they were up to, working unsupervised in the kitchen could be dangerous. Hopefully their idea of brunch was Pop Tarts and cereal. Anything else and it might take a firehouse rescue team to resuscitate Logan.

CHAPTER SIXTEEN

Dread stirred in Logan's stomach. Anyone would think he was about to open the door to the lion's den. Anxious, he turned the knob to find the door locked. "This can't be good."

Delicate fingers gently patted his arm. "Relax. Knock or ring the doorbell."

"You're right." He opted to ring the bell.

Within seconds, the front door slowly opened. To his surprise, not only was Michelle standing inside waiting for them, she wore a bright smile and held her arm in front of her with the kitchen towel draped over her forearm. "Welcome to Chez Miller." Her other arm let go of the door knob and waved them in. "Please be seated."

His gaze followed the direction of her hand to see the small dinette table had been set for two. Taking hold of Leah's hand, he slowly followed his daughter to the table.

"Oh, this is just lovely." Leah grinned at Michelle.

Stunned at the beautiful table setting, it took Logan a moment to react and pull out Leah's chair. When he glanced at his daughter, she winked and mouthed *good job, Daddy*.

Placing her napkin on her lap, Leah scanned the setting. "I've never had orange juice in a wine glass before, but it's pretty."

"And safe." He sighed. "I guess you were right."

"It's a little dark." Trish appeared with an adult apron tied around her, the hem almost to the floor, and a dish of toast in hand.

"This looks delicious." Leah smiled at the little girl, beaming with pride.

Though not quite charcoal, the edges were definitely on

the verge of dark enough to be considered charred. "Thank you, sweetie." He reached for the butter and Trish sighed.

"I told Michelle we didn't need to push the button twice."

"This is perfect." Leah didn't even bother with the butter, she simply took a bite and muttered, "Yum."

Trish smiled. "I'll be right back with the coffee."

"Coffee?" Logan leaned forward, speaking softly to not be heard in the kitchen.

"Coffee pots aren't that hard, really," Leah whispered back.

He leaned back and sighed. Leah was being more level-headed than he was. "I suppose."

A sudden crashing noise came from the kitchen and Logan scooted his chair back.

Grabbing his hand to stop him, Leah shook her head. "Things fall. Give it a minute."

He didn't like that advice one bit, but she was probably right. Especially when a small voice shouted from the kitchen, "Just another minute!" He figured, if they could yell from one room to the other, no one was dying.

"Wonder what they dropped?" Leah took a sip of her juice.

A moment later, Michelle came through the kitchen doorway, a cup in each hand, her steps slow and deliberate, focusing on not spilling. When she reached the table and placed the two mugs down, her relieved sigh could most likely have been heard all the way at the Baron ranch. "I'll be right back with cream and sugar."

She trotted happily to the kitchen and returned with a quart of milk and the sugar bowl. So much for elegance. Nonetheless, the effort made him smile. As soon as he stirred the sugar in, a flurry of grinds floated to the top.

The abundance of grinds in Leah's cup were more visible against the milky backdrop. "I suspect someone forgot the filter."

Logan braved a sip, swallowed hard and tried not to wince. "That's my vote."

"Oh, foo," came softly from the kitchen.

"Do you think they realized the mistake with the coffee grinds?" He didn't really want to stew over what else they might be doing in the kitchen on their own.

"Don't know, but it does seem they're having a bit of a challenge in there." Leah's eyes suddenly filled with light. He could almost see a light bulb turning on over her head. "Give me your coffee."

"What? Why?" What on earth could she want to do with it? "You certainly can't drink mine too."

"Agreed." Her gaze shot over her shoulder and then quickly she stood with the two mugs and hurried to the opposite side of the living room, then poured most of each cup into the potted plant by the patio door. He had to give her credit, weren't coffee grinds good for plants? The milk and sugar he wasn't so sure about, but he was fairly sure it would sit better with the plants than their stomachs.

"Thanks."

"What else are friends for?"

Friends. Though he'd like to think they were on the road to much more, he liked being her friend too. Too many couples skipped that step for a solid foundation.

"Ouch," what sounded like Michelle, cried out softly from the kitchen.

"Now can I go see?" It took all his self-control to ask Leah and not just run to the kitchen.

Just as she opened her mouth to speak, a strong whiff of burning something carried into the room, followed by the piercing screech of a smoke alarm, and Trish's loud cry, "Daddy!"

Kicking her seat back, Leah looked him in the eye. "Now!"

Leah actually beat Logan into the kitchen by several strides. Every single inch of the kitchen, from the counters to the floors, was covered in white powder. Trish sat on the floor on a massive mound of flour. To her right, the oven door was wide open with fire spewing up. Any second she could see the entire kitchen going up in flames.

"Holy…" Logan came to a stop behind her before pivoting around Michelle at the sink and darting across the small space, he slammed the door shut.

"Daddy, the bacon!" Michelle screeched, holding her thumb under the water. "Don't step on the bacon!"

Step on? By now, Leah had dropped to the floor and cradled Trish in her arms, searching lightly for any signs of cuts or burns. "Are you hurt?"

"No. But the eggs." She pointed to the fridge. Two cartons of eggs were on the ground with gooey yellow liquid pooled around it and slowly running toward the island. What a mess.

The island cabinet doors banged open and Logan pulled out a small fire extinguisher.

Thank heaven; she wouldn't have had a clue where to find it, or the free hands. "Come on, baby, we need to get out of this mess. You too, Michelle."

"But the bacon," Michelle muttered around a thumb that she'd stuck in her mouth.

At least Leah knew what the earlier *ouch* was for. She tried to stand without losing her hold on the young girl or sliding across the floor. From the corner of her eyes as she pushed carefully to her feet, a flash of yellow polo shirt flew past and disappeared, followed by the painful sound of the human body slamming against the hard tile floor. "Oh, hell."

Now both girls ran across the kitchen to where their dad laid sprawled out flat on the floor, the extinguisher at his side.

"Daddy!" Michelle cried and reached for a pan on the floor.

"Don't touch that!" Leah shouted. The bacon was scattered across the small area along with some grease, but most of it was still in the hot pan. "You can burn yourself. Both of you carefully go sit in the living room."

Squatting over Logan, she glanced up to see if the oven was still on fire. One good thing about fires, if you cut off oxygen, they die out faster than a rose in winter. Looking down at Logan, she scanned him quickly, thankful not to see any blood. "Logan?"

"Ugghh," a low gravely moan reached her ears.

"Don't move," she ordered.

Lifting his hand to the side of his head, his eyes tightly shut, he softly muttered, "Wouldn't think of it."

"Did you hit your head?"

One eye sprang open.

"Never mind. Dumb question." She gently ran her hands down his arms to his wrists, then leaned over to look at his ankles for any signs of sprains or a break. "Does anything hurt beside your head?"

It took so long for him to answer, she almost thought he wasn't going to. "I don't think so."

That was a relief. Taking an inner deep breath, she smiled down at him. "We really do have to stop meeting in the kitchen like this, but at least this time there's no blood."

"Cute," he chuckled before grimacing. Opening both eyes, he strained to a sitting position.

"I don't think you should move. You can never be too careful with a head injury. Let me call an ambulance."

"For a bump," hand at the base of his head again, and wincing through clenched teeth, he blew out a sigh, "on the head?"

"Yes. An ambulance will get you straight in to see a doctor without spending hours waiting. You stay put. I'm calling."

"No."

"Yes."

Tilting his head slightly, he opened one eye and focused on her. "I'm not going to win this, am I?"

She shook her head.

Gritting his teeth, he grabbed her hand. "Don't you think calling an ambulance is just a bit over the top for a slip and fall? Let's clean up the girls. Make sure they're okay, then you can drive me to the doctor."

"Hospital."

"Whatever." His shoulders slumped. "Deal?"

"Okay. But you stay here. I'll check the girls more closely and then we'll all go. But the ambulance would have been faster."

He chuckled at her persistence. "At least I've agreed to the hospital even if I really don't need to go."

"I'm sure that's what every famous person who bumped their head then died said to their loved ones too."

"Loved ones." A lazy smile replaced the frown on his forehead.

She had an overwhelming urge to lean over and kiss the boo-boo away the same as her mother had done with all the kids when they were growing up. If only all of this were just that simple.

CHAPTER SEVENTEEN

One thing was sure, Logan needed to set down some new ground rules for his daughters in the kitchen. He wasn't sure what he slipped on, but the most likely culprit was the grease on the floor from where Michelle had dropped the tray of bacon. He hated to think what would have happened if they had tried to fry the bacon in a pan.

"How you doing?" Leah came through the standard ER blue drawn curtains. "Claire took the children to the ranch."

"I thought she was going to stay with them at the apartment?"

"She was. Till she saw the kitchen. The girls wanted to finish cooking and then clean up. Devlin suggested that was a mess for professionals and he'd call to make sure it got done quickly. So Claire waited for Devlin's cleaning crew and then took the kids to the ranch. I'm pretty sure there's going to be some additional lessons on kitchen safety."

"What I don't understand is, how did they set the oven on fire?"

"Marshmallows."

"What?"

"Michelle had the bacon on the lower rack and a tray with graham crackers and marshmallows on the top rack. If you didn't know, marshmallows are quite flammable."

"Why was she cooking graham crackers and marshmallows?"

"S'mores."

"For brunch?" He was fairly confident that his confusion had nothing to do with the throbbing bump on his head.

"They like S'mores. To a nine-year-old, brunch has no limits."

He'd have shaken his head if it wasn't still throbbing. "I can't believe I'm imposing on your family again."

"It's not an imposition." Her gaze landed on the metal table at his side. "What's that?"

Slowly turning his head, he sighed. "Ice pack."

Her brows rose high on her forehead. "Are you supposed to be putting that where you hit your head?"

"For something like fifteen minutes on and fifteen minutes off."

"And how long has it been off?"

This was what he was trying to avoid. He'd held it to his aching head for a while but simply wasn't in the mood to keep it up. "A while."

"That's what I thought." She reached for the traditional ice bag and just as she brought it close, his hand closed around hers.

"Thank you."

"You're welcome." Her gaze remained locked with his and she didn't let go of the ice. "You scared me."

"Not my intention." Careful not to rattle his head, he pushed to a more upright position, grabbing her hand when she pulled back. "Stay close."

Settling in on the small space between him and the edge of the bed, it was easy to see the worry in her eyes. "Have the doctors said anything yet?"

"No. But I've had every scan under the sun."

"I couldn't get the nurses to tell me anything. Finally got frustrated and called the Governor. A few minutes later the same nurse brought me back here."

"I'm sorry. There's no reason you couldn't have been waiting in here with me instead of out there."

"That's what I said, but," her head cocked back and forth and her voice went all nasally, "I'm sorry, only immediate family or MPAs are allowed inside with the patients."

"MPA?"

"Medical Power of Attorney. Which, I know this isn't

the right time, but your girls are your next of kin but obviously not old enough to make health decisions. Do you have a designated MPA?"

"You'd think after losing Deb so unexpectedly, I'd have taken care of things like that, but I'm sorry to say, I haven't."

Her face crumpled as she made a tsking noise. "We're going to have to organize you better. My grandfather always said a plan in place will stop Murphy cold."

"What?" Normally he was able to follow her train of thought, but right now he was lost.

"Murphy's law. If something can go wrong, it will. The Governor believes if you have a plan in place for when things go wrong, then they won't go wrong. Sort of like bringing an umbrella with you so it doesn't rain, because if you forget it at home…"

"It will rain." Somehow that made perfect sense. Now whether that implied he was meant to be with a Baron or that he'd hit his head harder than he thought, he couldn't say.

"So," she leaned forward and retrieved the ice bag again, "let's start here."

"Yes, ma'am." If all it took to make her smile was to use the dang ice bag, then he'd suffer through the cold.

Leah proceeded to tell him how she'd spoken more in depth with her sister Claire about the grocery store trip and learned that there very likely could have been three five pound bags of flour scattered across the floor. Also that it never occurred to Claire when the girls mentioned wanting to make S'mores, that they couldn't be cooked in the oven. By the time Leah was done retelling the conversations, they were both laughing themselves silly.

"Excuse me." The ER doctor who had ordered the initial tests when he first came in, stood on the opposite side of his bed. "I've got some results back."

"And?" Leah squeezed his hand more tightly.

"The official diagnosis is you have a bump on the head."

The power in Leah's grip eased and she blew out a long

breath. "No concussion."

The doctor shook his head. "I still would like someone to stay with you tonight and check every couple of hours that you can wake up."

"Done." Leah answered before Logan could respond that he lived alone with his two young daughters.

All he could think of as the doctor rambled on about who knew what, was that this entire day would have gone very differently if he hadn't had Leah there when it all went down. For all he knew, by the time he'd confirmed that Trish was not physically injured, the flames might have spread to the rest of the kitchen, and most likely to the adjoining apartments. The day could have gone so wrong. As far as he was concerned, he didn't want to learn to live again without her. Even on a perfect day, when everything went right, having Leah at his side made the day even better. Somehow, he had to make sure he didn't lose her.

Leah couldn't believe what an absolutely crazy day today had turned out to be. Waking up to donuts, hot coffee, and Logan had been the best start to her morning. Then the curious twist of a crayon written invitation from Michelle and Trish, that had been awfully sweet.

"You have to admit," Logan unlocked the front door of his apartment, "if this had been a reality show, we'd have been at the top of the viewing charts."

"If I'd had my phone handy, your sliding dive would have been great for that funny video TV show."

"I thought the flames shooting out of the oven was a ratings grabber."

A slow chuckle tickled her throat. "The flour mound on the ground was definitely unique."

Logan sank into the sofa, leaning his head back on the over-stuffed piece of furniture and chuckling softly. "Didn't your sister wonder what the heck the girls needed fifteen pounds of flour for?"

Knowing Claire the way she did, she couldn't help but laugh a little louder. "My sister has always known her way around animals, barns, and stables. As long as there were no horses in the kitchen, you weren't going to find Claire in there."

His shoulders shook with laughter. "But fifteen pounds? The worst cook in the world would have to know nothing requires fifteen pounds of flour to bake. Unless you're cooking for the entire Marine Corps."

"Hey." She sputtered with laughter, thinking about the absolute mess they'd walked into. "You're preaching to the choir. I don't bake, but I'd like to think I would have redirected some of the purchases." She leaned forward to push to her feet. "I should go see how Devlin's people left the kitchen."

Without moving his head, he extended his arm and took hold of her hand. "Stay. We can check the kitchen later."

Who was she to argue with a good plan? Leaning back beside him, she squeezed his hand.

"Tell me something." His eyes drifted closed.

"You must be tired. Maybe you should go get a nap. I promise to check on you in an hour or two."

Logan shook his head. "I'm fine. Just thinking."

"You sure?"

He nodded. "Are you a romantic?"

"I think every woman is at least a little bit of a romantic."

Turning his head to face her, he pulled her hand and flattened it over his heart. "Do you feel that?"

She nodded. His heart was beating as fast as hers.

"You do that to me."

Five simple words and they brought a slow smile to her face.

"You deserve the best this world has to offer. You deserve roses, and champagne, and tuxedos, and a man down on one knee flashing you with a beautiful flawless diamond that's as perfect as you are."

"I'm far from perfect and I don't need diamonds."

"You at least deserve the effort." He closed his eyes and

breathed. "I want you to know my intentions, because if you don't think some day you would be open to sharing my world, my family, my life, as my wife, then I need to know now. If you're okay with it, then one day, when the time is right and my head isn't threatening to split open, I'm going to get down on that one knee with champagne and a diamond and officially ask you to let me love you for the rest of my life."

With each word in his declaration, her heart kicked up and beat faster and faster. When he uttered his last word, her rapidly beating heart nearly melted in her chest.

"I'm sorry if I'm rushing you." Despite the headache, he straightened and leaned forward, enfolding her clasped hand in both of his. "Is there any chance for me?"

All she could manage was a nod. Her mouth had gone dry and her heart had turned to mush. Mustering up every bit of strength she had, she forced her lips to move and her vocal cords to speak. "Yes."

Relief visibly washed over his face. "I promise to do my best to be patient."

She shook her head. "I don't think you understand. I said yes."

His eyes narrowed with confusion.

"Yes to your world, your family, your life and to being your wife. I don't need tuxedos, champagne, or diamonds. I don't even need you to get down on one knee. I love you, Logan Miller, and I love your daughters, and when you slipped on that floor today and for just a minute I thought you were hurt, I hurt too. Whenever you're ready, so am I."

A smile as wide as the Brazos River spread across his face. Sliding over, he pulled her into the crux of his shoulder and planted a sweet, adoring, and breathtaking kiss on her. When he pulled back, he reached into a pocket and pulled out a five-dollar bill, then slipping it into her grasp and folding her fingers closed in both his hands, he leveled his gaze with hers. "I know you're worth a million times more, but how do you feel about a spring wedding?"

EPILOGUE

A typical Saturday afternoon at the Baron family homestead, a good number of the clan gathered on the veranda and scattered around the rolling yard. Some played horseshoes, others played corn hole, but most were merely lounging about the veranda.

Rachel, seated beside her husband and totally at home with her new role as wife, held Dylan's hand, while her free hand sketched invisible lines in the air. With every word as she described in almost painful detail her latest restoration efforts, Rachel's eyes sparkled with passion. That same passion was reflected in Dylan's gaze as he watched his wife, though there was little doubt in Claire's mind that his interest had nothing to do with architecture and everything to do with his bride.

In the distance, Leah jumped high in the air, hooted loud enough to wake their ancestors from the dead, then spun around, throwing herself at her husband. The way Logan scooped her into his arms, twirled her around, and then planted a brief but sweet kiss on her lips, would have made a fabulous commercial for Valentine's day gifts. Even his daughters noticed, laughing and giggling and clearly happy with their dad's new wife.

New wife. Boy, did those words rattle Claire's mind. Of course, she and every other sibling expected to some day find Mr. or Miss Right, marry, and eventually have children. Claire simply hadn't expected two of her sisters to fall back to back and one of them to inherit an instant family. Though, frankly, motherhood seemed to fit the lawyer well. Who knew? Watching the family laugh and tease in the distance until Logan and the girls broke out in a game of catch me if you can with Leah happily running behind her new daughters sent a surge of love, and even pride, at her sister's new life, through her like wildfire.

"Almost hate to break up the fun." Hazel stepped up beside them, holding a cloth-covered tray.

"Ooh." Claire sniffed the air like a bloodhound. "What have we there?"

Hazel shifted the tray away from Claire. "Fixings for S'mores."

"The girls will love that." Grams nodded her approval. "Besides, we need to hammer home that S'mores are meant for outdoor cooking."

"Amen to that," Claire agreed. When she took in the sight of the kitchen turned war zone, she'd almost had a heart attack. She couldn't begin to fathom what it must have been like for her sister to walk into that, and with the oven on fire to boot.

"I thought I heard Leah mention that the girls wanted to go horseback riding after the game of corn hole." Porter took a sip of his longneck beer.

"Getting late." The Governor looked up at the dusky sky. "Better save it for another day. Wouldn't want anyone falling off a horse in the dark."

"Or daylight." A mischievous glint in his eye, Cooper stifled a smile and glared at his brother. "Fallen off any horses lately?"

"Ha ha," Devlin snipped at his brother. "Get caught in any fences lately?"

"Touche," Cooper shrugged.

"All right, boys," their grandmother chastised.

"Are you boys causing trouble again?" Mitch came up behind his cousins, his very pregnant wife at his side.

"Have my seat." Cooper popped up at the same time Devlin and Porter shot up from their seats.

All the men literally stumbling over themselves to give Gwyneth a seat had Claire chuckling. She could just imagine what these guys would be like when their own wives, someday, were nine months pregnant and ready to pop at any moment.

"Look, Aunt Claire." Trish came running up, waving a clover in the air. "Daddy says they bring good luck."

Behind the little girl, her sister Michelle came hurrying up the hill to stop at her side. Not far behind, Leah and Logan followed their children.

Gwyneth eased, slowly, onto the Adirondack chair, landing with an oomph.

"When is the baby coming?" Michelle asked.

Mitch's wife tapped her hand on her belly. "Soon, I hope."

"Can we feel the baby move again?" Now both girls stood at either side of Gwyneth like sentries.

From what Claire had been told, the young girls were fascinated with the idea of a baby ever since Gwyneth had let them feel the future Baron moving about.

"Can we have one?" Trish spun around to face Leah and Logan.

The Governor and Grams seemed to sit up at attention all of a sudden. Claire didn't blame them, she was more than curious to see how the newlyweds reacted.

Holding hands, Logan sighed at his daughter. "Sweetie…"

"You said that there has to be a mommy and a daddy to have a baby. Now we have both." The little girl grinned over at Leah with the toothiest smile Claire had ever seen.

"Oh, well…" Logan's brows rose high over his eyes as he looked to Leah for help.

All Leah had to offer was a lazy one shoulder shrug.

Claire found herself watching the two interact like she would a tennis match. Next, Logan tipped his head to one side and then Leah shrugged both shoulders. The two spoke silently until nodding, Logan turned to his girls. "We'll talk about this later."

The two harrumphed, but returned to their fascination with Gwyneth's well-rounded belly.

It took all of Claire's self-discipline not to jump up and applaud. Not only had her sister and her new husband learned the art of silent communication, but Claire was pretty sure there had been some silent agreement to add a baby to the family. Wouldn't that be fabulous?

With all the ladies in the family comfortably seated around the fire pit, and all the men gathered to one side chatting, Claire couldn't think of anything more perfect. Soon the next generation of Barons would begin to arrive and the world would be even sweeter. Too bad none of this was in her immediate future. Her veterinarian business kept her awfully busy. Maybe one of these days a single cat owner would come in, take one look at her, and fall head over boot heels for the lady vet. Most likely, a good man was not going to fall into her lap and she simply didn't have time to go looking. Too bad, the idea of hearth and home was beginning to grow on her. Really too bad.

Enjoy an excerpt from
Just One Rodeo

"It's time!" Claire Baron's vet tech shouted from the hallway.

Checking on one of her post-op patients still sleeping off the anesthesia, Claire gave the sweet cattle dog a pat on the head and strolled over to the doorway. She was positive she'd cancelled all morning appointments for the emergency surgery, and couldn't figure what the woman was shouting about. Sticking her head into the hall, she looked for her tech. "Time for what?"

"For what?" Kathy came hurrying down the hall from the front, grinning wider than a lottery winner. "The baby!"

Baby. Claire blinked and then recognition dawned. So consumed with the injured dog, she'd forgotten the entire family was on baby watch for her cousin Mitch and his wife. "How long has she been in labor?" Claire slipped out of her lab coat and quickly hung it on a nearby hook.

"Rachel didn't tell me."

Claire hurried down the hall to her office, Kathy right on her heels. "What about the contractions? How far apart are they?"

Kathy shook her head. "I don't know."

Grabbing her purse from the desk drawer, Claire leveled her gaze with Kathy. "Water broke?"

Shoulders lifted in a shrug at the same time Kathy's hands flipped up in an *I don't know* gesture.

Biting back her frustration at limited information, Claire slammed the drawer shut and smiled up at Kathy. "What exactly did Rachel say?"

"Gwyneth is in labor and your presence has been

requested at the ranch ASAP."

Her purse slung over her shoulder, Claire gave up digging for her truck keys and snapped her head up. "Me? Why me?"

"You are a trained medical professional." Kathy shrugged again.

"Yeah, for four legged critters, not humans. I don't do humans."

Kathy chuckled. "Relax. It sounds like the call went out far and wide. If it makes you feel any better, Rachel mentioned that CJ was already on the way."

That did help. A trained nurse, CJ would be way more helpful in this situation than Claire would. "Okay. I know first babies are notoriously slow, but since we have no idea if she's been laboring for ten minutes or ten hours, I'm heading out to the ranch as summoned. When Gail comes back from lunch, tell her to cancel the remainder of my appointments for the day."

"Will do." Kathy nodded. "And please keep us posted."

"Deal." Hurrying back up the hall, she suddenly remembered her post-op patient and, stuttering to a stop, spun about. "The dog."

Kathy waved her back around. "Go. I'll keep an extra eye on him. Even sleep with him if I have to. Just don't forget to call with updates." Kathy's hands fisted in front of her and she practically shook with excitement. "This is so much fun. We're having a baby!"

Something told Claire that if it were Kathy having the baby, she wouldn't use the word fun.

Pushing the pedal to the metal, Claire turned on the music and picked her favorite artist, blaring full blast. They were having a baby. The first in the family. She was so darn excited anyone would think it was Claire or one of her sisters who was about to become a mother. Gwyneth had only been a Baron for a little more than a year, but it felt like she'd always been part of the family, making this event so exciting for everyone. After all, Gwyneth wasn't laboring at home, she was at the ranch. Mitch had insisted on having her surrounded by family and Gwyneth was all for it.

Another example of how the woman had embraced being a Baron.

At the same time she'd pulled onto the property, a line of cars pulled in behind her, adding to the row of cars already parked along the curved drive. Apparently the entire clan had indeed been called.

Inside, siblings and cousins were scattered about. Some in the living room seated, others pacing, others in the kitchen making sandwiches and coffee with Hazel. The excitement was running so high that the air almost crackled with it.

"How long has she been in labor?" Claire addressed the women in the kitchen.

Hazel flipped her wrist. "We think her back ache last night was the beginning. Gwyneth woke up this morning grumbling and disinterested in breakfast. That's when I knew."

"When did she know?" Claire asked.

Hazel shrugged. "When I told her. We called the doula right away. She's upstairs with the midwife."

That's right. Claire had almost forgotten that Gwyneth had not only wanted to labor at home, but that she had decided against the midwife's birthing center at the hospital and wanted to have the baby in the comfort of a home. Rubbing her hands together, Claire joined the pacers in the living room. Now all she had to do was hurry up and wait.

Spectators filled the towering grandstands in the dusty small town arena. The scents of leather and hay mingled with the faint aroma of barbecue drifting in from the nearby concessions. For Tucker, all of it smelled like heaven. Slapping his hat on his thigh and placing it back on his head, he took a quick glance around. He didn't have to hear the rising hum of voices to know the air was thick with anticipation for tonight's events—he could feel it all around him like a warm blanket. Right along with an edge of excitement, just enough to have him and his best horse, Thunder, eager to nail this last event. After another long year on the circuit, if he and Sam could keep up the points for the next couple of events, they'd have what they needed to send him and Sam to the grand finals and the top prize he'd coveted all season.

Tucker glanced over at his longtime friend and partner in team roping. Sam reminded him of the stereotypical cowboy. His face rugged with weathered features, and a perpetual twinkle in his eye. The man's easy smile belied the years of hard work and dedication he'd poured into the rodeo circuit. This would be their year. Tucker could feel it in his bones, right along side every bump and bruise. Thunder was the best damn horse a man could ask for, and Sam's horse Rocky was a close second.

His Stetson pulled low over his brow as he surveyed the scene before them, Sam bobbed his head and sported a lazy, contented smile. "You ready to take this home?"

Tucker nodded. "More than ready. All we have to do is stay on our horses and we're in like Flynn."

Sam snorted a knowing chuckle, as if either of them would fall of a horse that wasn't bucking.

Coming toward them, a man and two young boys focused on Tucker and Thunder. When they were close enough to hear the conversation over the hum of the crowds, one kid spat *it's him,* and the other hollered back, *is not*. The bickering brothers made him smile, remembering the same one upmanship between him and his brother. In the end, the father leaned over, nodded, and must have uttered the magic words because both boys looked thoroughly reproved and appropriately contrite. As they walked by, one raised his head and his thumb. "We're rooting for you, Tucker. You and Thunder."

"Much obliged." He tipped his hat to the boys. Still a bit startled whenever someone recognized him, or, like the boys, actually followed his career. The whole concept of being well known in the circuit caught him off guard every time.

As a young boy he'd followed his favorite rodeo riders

and dreamed of the day he could win the buckle himself. After all, at the age of six, what boy cared about money? It was the shiny buckle that held his dreams. Some days he couldn't believe his life had become a dream come true. At least that would be the case if the finals went as well as this season. Too many other days, he awoke with the standard aches and pains and knew his days on the circuit were numbered. This *had* to be his year.

He carefully watched the team in the arena do their thing. A late start here or a missed rope toss there, Tucker knew all too well how much the slightest misstep could cost in the rankings.

Mounted and ready for their turn, their hats pulled low over their brows, Tucker and Sam guided their horses into position on either side of the steer's gate. Tucker's grip tightened on the reins, his gaze locked on the pen where the animals waited. Sam exuded calm confidence, and focused concentration as he readied his rope, set to ride like the proverbial wind.

Tucker felt a surge of adrenaline course through his veins as the announcer's voice boomed over the loudspeaker, signaling the start of their run. This was their moment, their chance to shine beneath the bright lights of the rodeo arena. Tucker urged Thunder forward, the powerful horse surging into action with effortless grace. The wind whipped around Tucker as they thundered across the arena, the rhythm of Thunder's hooves echoing in perfect sync with the pounding of Tucker's heart.

In the blink of an eye, they closed in on their target—a lone steer racing ahead. Focused on the task at hand, Tucker's pulse quickened, his senses sharpening with each passing second. With practiced precision, Sam expertly wielded his lasso, the rope whirling overhead before settling around the steer's horns with pinpoint accuracy. The steer kicked its rear legs, twisting around its movements tempered by the ropes that bound it.

Tucker's breath came in exhilarated gasps as he swung his rope, the loop sailing through the air in a graceful arc before settling around the steer's hind leg. A chorus of cheers erupted from the crowd. With the steer now securely roped at both ends, Tucker and Sam exchanged a knowing glance, a silent acknowledgment of their synchronized skill and unwavering teamwork. Needed points secured, he bobbed his head, loosening his grip on the ropes and letting the steer hurry away. They'd done it. Their fastest time of the evening. One step closer to finals, he knew they'd make it as surely as he knew his name was Tucker John Pride.

Read more of Just One Rodeo available now

MEET CHRIS

USA TODAY Bestselling Author of dozens of contemporary novels, including the award winning Aloha Series, Chris Keniston lives in suburban Dallas with her husband, two human children, and two canine children. Though she loves her puppies equally, she admits being especially attached to her German Shepherd rescue. After all, even dogs deserve a happily ever after.

More on Chris and all her books can be found at
www.chriskeniston.com

Follow Chris' Monday Blog at her website
ChrisKenistonAuthor

Follow Chris on Facebook at
ChrisKenistonAuthor

Never miss a New Release!
Sign up for News from Chris:
www.chriskeniston.com/newsletter.html

Questions? Comments?
I would love to hear from you! You can reach me at:
chris@chriskeniston.com

www.ingramcontent.com/pod-product-compliance
Lightning Source LLC
Chambersburg PA
CBHW021157010826
48971CB00014B/2625